SAKĪNA'S KĪSS

Praise for *Ghachar Ghochar*:

'One of the finest literary works you will ever encounter . . . Literary perfection is elusive, yet it is possible, as Vivek Shanbhag demonstrates in his magnificent novella, where comedy is undercut by seething menace and overwhelming regret at a failure to act decently.' Eileen Battersby, *Irish Times*

'This tragicomic novella is both a classic tale of wealth and moral ruin and a parable about capitalism and Indian society.' *New Yorker*

'A story that packs a powerful punch . . . "What can I say – it is one of the strengths of families to pretend that they desire what is unavoidable." So perfectly put is this last line, it belongs up there with the now infamous opening of *Anna Karenina*, the clipped, exact prose of Perur's translation nevertheless ably conveying the rich depth of meaning therein . . . Shanbhag is the real deal, this gem of a novel resounding with chilling truths.' *Independent*

'A remarkable novel about the fragile civilities of bourgeois life. The reader becomes absorbed in the unforgiving self-knowledge and expansive humanity contained in every page.' Amit Chaudhuri

'*Ghachar Ghochar* presents life and its undercurrents with limpid prose and quiet insight.' Yiyun Li

'Vivek Shanbhag is an Indian Chekhov, illuminating the romantic and financial tensions in middle-class urban India with a doctor's precision and sensitivity.' Suketu Mehta

'What's most impressive about *Ghachar Ghochar* is how much intricacy and turmoil gets distilled into its few pages. Vivek Shanbhag, who writes in the South Indian language Kannada and is translated here by Srinath Perur into clean, conversational English, is a master of inference and omission . . . There's a deeper loneliness in this wise and skillful book that no covering can conceal.' *Wall Street Journal*

'As always, fiction encapsulates a kind of truth with an immediacy and vividness that no amount of data and historical summaries can begin to approach. In just over a hundred pages *Ghachar Ghochar* distils the human soul's infinitely complicated relationship with money. Without Srinath Perur's precisely fluent and beautiful English translation, this jewel of a novel would have been little known even in India.' Neel Mukherjee, *Times Literary Supplement*

'This spiny, scary story of moral decline, crisply plotted and no thicker than my thumb, has been heralded as the finest Indian novel in a decade.' *New York Times*

VIVEK SHANBHAG

SAKINA'S KISS

Translated from the Kannada by
SRINATH PERUR

faber

First published in this edition in 2025
by Faber & Faber Ltd
The Bindery, 51 Hatton Garden
London ECIN 8HN

Published in the Kannada as *Sakinala Muttu*
by Akshara Prakashana 2021

A CIP record for this book
is available from the British Library

ISBN 978-0-571-39083-0

Printed and bound in the UK on FSC® certified paper in line with our continuing
commitment to ethical business practices, sustainability and the environment.
For further information see faber.co.uk/environmental-policy

Our authorised representative in the EU for product safety is
Easy Access System Europe, Mustamäe tee 50, 10621 Tallinn, Estonia
gpsr.requests@easproject.com

10 9 8 7 6 5 4 3 2 1

For Deepa

'Things cannot be understood in the here and now.'

Allama Prabhu, twelfth-century mystic poet

1

'There are no coincidences, only unseen chains of consequence.'

The line I had scrawled on the last page of a notebook caught my eye. I was in the bedroom, searching for the visiting card a carpenter had given me the previous day, but finding just about everything else. Actually, my half-hearted rummaging hardly amounted to searching. It was like this whenever I tried to find something – I would dig up everything I had preserved over the years and lose myself. If I came upon an old, folded newspaper, I would go through the whole thing trying to recall why I had kept it. I'd find a group photo from a long-ago training workshop and muse about how my appearance had changed over the years. When I found investment forms I had never got around to filling, I immediately set about calculating what the missed opportunity had cost.

Years ago, I used to write down lines that I could quote when the occasion presented itself. These still surfaced from time to time on scraps of paper or in dusty writing pads. Now that I had found this gem, I went to the kitchen to read it out to Viji.

It was around seven on a Saturday evening. Viji, almost done with cooking, was wiping the counter with one eye on the rasam boiling on the stove. I entered the kitchen and said, 'Listen to this.'

'Later. First, give me a hand here,' she said. There was an unmistakable weariness in her tone that seemed to say, 'You and your quotations.'

I ignored her, raised the notebook theatrically and said, 'Okay, listen carefully now.' It wouldn't have escaped her that I was forcing her to pay attention.

Before she could retaliate, there was the sound of knocking at the front door. I was surprised – who knocks when there is a bell to ring? I put the notebook down on the kitchen counter and went to the door. First, I cast a quick eye over the hall to see how it might appear to a visitor. I straightened a chair, gathered the strewn sheets of a newspaper and, wondering how it had got there, picked up a used napkin lying on the sofa. I hurriedly looked for a place to hide it but none suggested itself. With my foot I slid aside all the footwear left at the entrance and opened the door halfway, concealing the napkin behind it in my left hand.

Two young men in jeans stood outside. One of them, wearing a white T-shirt, seemed to be around twenty. His hair glistened with the gel he had used to shape it to a crest. The other looked a little older. He had coarse, somewhat tousled hair and was wearing a blue shirt with rolled-up sleeves. Their manner was tentative, as if they wanted to say something but did not know how to begin. Since they resembled the people Viji called to fix our forever clogged kitchen sink, I motioned to them to wait and was heading back to the kitchen when one of them called out: 'Sir . . . sir!'

The boy in the blue shirt said, 'We are Rekha's friends.'

My expression must have changed on hearing my daughter's name. The two attempted to summon deferential smiles. I came to the door again. 'She is not at home,' I said.

'Oh. Where is she?'

'She's gone to the village.'

'When will she be back?'

'No idea.'

'Can we come in?'

'What is this about?'

'We wanted to talk for a couple of minutes.'

'Yes, tell me.'

'Just two minutes.'

I opened the door fully and stepped back. 'Come in,' I said, trying not to let my annoyance show.

They entered and sat down next to each other on the ebony sofa. I took the chair opposite. On the glass-top table between us lay the day's English paper, which I had just folded. On its lower shelf was a small stack of newspapers going back a week.

Blue-shirt seemed to be doing the talking. He asked, 'Can we reach Rekha by phone?'

'Our house there has no landline or mobile signal,' I said. 'The only way to talk to her is if she calls from the town. Now, tell me who you are.'

My answer appeared to reassure them for some reason. Blue-shirt said, 'That's what we thought. Her phone is switched off, and she isn't replying to messages either. This is her friend. They're classmates. BA final year. I'm their senior.'

I worked out that if he was senior to final-year students, he must no longer be in college.

'It's to discuss next term's project work. How can we reach her?'

'I told you. It's she who has to call. When she does, I'll tell her.'

'Actually it's a bit urgent.'

'As I said, son, it is she who has to call. What is your name?' I asked the question in a tone that betrayed my irritation.

He pointed to the boy sitting next to him. 'This is Manjuprakash. His friends call him MP3, so that's the name you'll have to use. Please ask her to call him. She has his number. I'm Rajkumar – RK. It's enough to mention his name.'

'All right, I'll tell her,' I said, without enthusiasm.

MP3 had a bewildered air about him. All this while he had neither made eye contact nor spoken. Now, as if he had heard nothing that had been said so far, he blurted out: 'When is she returning?'

'Not anytime soon.' This was getting on my nerves. I tossed the napkin in my hand on to the empty chair next to me.

The two of them didn't seem to have anything more to say. My eyes drifted towards the books in the recessed cabinet next to the door. They ranged from *Learn C++* to books on kick-starting your career, setting your life on the right path in a single day and gaining valuable experience from the mistakes of others. Assorted knick-knacks took up space in between the books. In front of the cabinet were stacked two plastic chairs that we used to sit out on the balcony. An old cloth bag that we hung on the door for milk lay bunched up on the upper chair.

RK must have noticed my attention wander. 'We'll take your leave now, sir,' he said and stood up. MP3 followed him to the door.

As I was about to close the door, I thought I might have been needlessly stern with them. I sent them off with an amiable 'I'll definitely tell Rekha if she calls'. They took the stairs without waiting for the lift.

When I went to give my report to Viji, it turned out she had overheard the entire conversation. She said, stirring the rasam, 'How could you not realize? No way these boys want to talk about a project. They're obviously infatuated with her. Now the monkeys have found her phone switched off and come all the way here. It's the madness of boys that age. And you were telling them stories about the village.'

What she said made sense. I was annoyed with myself for not grasping the situation correctly. How could I have forgotten what my guru, Tiwari, had once whispered in my ear: 'Never say more than what is asked.'

Viji's face had the hint of a smile on it. 'Just don't give them the village address or the phone number of anyone there,' she said. 'Those idiots might jump on a motorcycle and set off.' She did not seem overly concerned, which reassured me somewhat.

Even so, I was no longer in the mood to force quotations on Viji. I picked up the notebook from the corner of the kitchen counter and went to the balcony to watch the boys leave.

Our third-floor flat's balcony is at the other end of the hall from the front door. The apartment building's gate and the road outside can be seen below to the right. I squinted into the fading light and saw ten to twelve boys passing through the gate. MP3 and RK must have been part of this larger group and had come up while their gang waited below. Now they all left together, walking with a stupid swagger.

I cannot stand such groups of boys. They roam around aimlessly instead of studying and waste their parents' money. They have no respect for elders or for rules and are a menace to society. The sight of them always sets off a small fury within me: the defiant way they carry themselves, those T-shirts and pointy hairstyles, their apathetic expressions. But when I try and put a finger on why I should feel that way, I cannot come up with a definite reason and it leaves me flustered.

I thought for a moment if I should tell Viji about the group. I called out to her from the balcony: 'Come here and look at this, Viji.' She was busy tempering, and by the time she came the boys were out of sight.

'It wasn't just the two of them. There was a big gang.'

'That's how boys come. Nothing to be afraid of.' She went back inside.

I followed her. 'I'm not afraid. So many boys have come home ever since she was in school, but no one has behaved like these two. They were hiding something. You should have seen them.'

'Oh, schoolboys are different, college boys are different. My college had boys like this too. It feels like nothing has changed in all these years except their clothes.'

'I don't know, I thought they were planning something. Now they know our house, they know she's away and they know me by face,' I said. RK's exaggerated politeness and MP3's shiftiness had made me suspicious. Viji entered the kitchen without saying anything.

Viji had once told me, 'Your true nature is to trust no one.' I don't agree. I think we should not rule out the presence of evil in our midst simply because we cannot see it. A little caution does no one any harm. It's possible that in certain areas Viji understands the mindset of the younger generation better than I do. She and Rekha fancy themselves a formidable debating team and turn on me when we have discussions at home. I accept defeat gracefully – in any case these are topics with little bearing on the real world. I am less charitable when it comes to politics.

But what was happening now was not a matter of idle discussion. We had a situation at our doorstep. As the man of the house, it was my duty to step forward and take care of it.

2

My name, Venkataramana, so richly intoned by the teachers at my village school, lost the flick of the tongue at its end in the mouths of my north Indian friends at engineering college and became Venkatraman. It then dwindled to Venkat among colleagues. If I had spent some time in the United States, I am sure I would have turned into a Venky. Perhaps the transformation of my name says something about the path I have travelled, and my easy acceptance of it something about the firmness of my convictions.

I had taken a picture of the family deity with me to engineering college, but it never emerged from my bag. A boy named Harish joined college the same day as me and neatly arranged pictures of gods and goddesses on his table. The students pounced on him with such glee that the nickname Bhatta – priest – stuck to him for the rest of his life. In the circumstances I thought it best to keep my god confined to my bag. After all, when you want to win a swimming race, you don't dive in carrying weights. For months I worried that someone might accidentally see the picture in my bag and spread the word. With all this going on I wasn't going to make a fuss about one syllable at the end of my name.

I finished my engineering and got a job at a multinational. On my first day at work, a smart alec from HR went on for two hours about company culture, reminding me every few minutes how fortunate I was to have got a job there. He sought my permission with a stale joke: 'You know, in an emergency it might be too late by the time your full name is said. Shall I call you Venkat?'

This reminded me of the custom of changing women's names after marriage, so I joked back: 'I feel like I am getting married to the job.'

He was too smart to get the joke. 'That is an amazing feeling,' he said and laughed. Then he took me around the office and introduced me to everyone as Venkat.

No one at home or in the village had called me anything other than Venkataramana, which also happens to be the name of our family deity. Every evening, at the end of her prayers, my mother sought the well-being of the family with an imploring 'Deva Venkataramana' that rings in my ears to this day. When colleagues started calling me Venkat, initially it felt as if my relationship with god too had somehow been diminished. But I got used to it soon enough.

Something I have not been able to come to terms with after all these years is the fact that my work has no connection to the electrical engineering I studied. Maybe I should not complain about this; after all, my salary grew steadily everywhere I worked.

Even then, I changed jobs from time to time, hoping to be a more important wheel in the organizational machinery. But no matter how attractive a position appeared from a distance, on drawing closer there were hundreds of wheels just like me. I have also struggled to make sense of just how many rungs of the ladder in a small company amount to a single rung in a large organization. Regular promotions have kept me from being entirely frustrated, but I have never been able to as much as glimpse the top of the ladder I set out to climb. Of late, I don't even clearly see where I can get off and retire.

Except in its details, the story of Viji's professional life is not very different from mine. She did her MSc in mathematics and got a job in the IT industry, which welcomes degree holders of all descriptions with open arms. Since it is hard to tell apart the various organisms that swim in the vast ocean of IT, I will not attempt to describe her role. But it should come as no surprise that her work too has no relation to the mathematics she studied. As a precaution against becoming obsolete, she signs up for courses every now and then to update her technical skills.

As a couple, we are not particularly good-looking, but we are not terribly unattractive either. We may not exactly be charismatic, but we are not off-putting. We both have a wheatish complexion, and if our physical attributes are considered, then my broad forehead and Viji's long, luxuriant hair might stand out. But such details are never noticed in the unexceptional, a point proved by the indifferent way in which the others who live in our apartment building know us only as 'the C-3 people'. The same neighbours, when talking about a particularly wealthy resident, say, 'Gupta, the tall man from the first floor.' The retired colonel on the second floor reminds them of the film star Shashi Kapoor.

To put it simply, if you averaged out various aspects of the lives of lakhs of people like ourselves, you might as well be describing us. Perhaps the only difference is that the cart of our particular existence is drawn by the twin oxen of both our incomes. This has allowed us to advance a step or two beyond the average. It gave us the courage, for instance, to take out a large home loan. We are a two-car household, even if they are small cars. We change our phones easily. We can go to restaurants and toss a card into the bill folder without thinking about it.

We believe our friends and relatives see us as successful. But no one spells out what exactly that means. They don't need to. It's common knowledge that the answers to a few simple questions give the measure of worldly progress. A house of one's own? If so, which area, who is the builder, how many BHK? Make of car? Kids? If so, which school? For people like us, who have successfully passed those milestones, there comes the test of being evaluated by the conduct and achievements of our children. That is where we stand now.

How have we continued to endure each other? If we were asked the sort of silly questions heard on TV shows that set out to find the ideal couple – his favourite colour, her first school's name – we would surely do well. But cracks below the surface of a relationship are harder to see. It is surprising that even in times like these no one has thought of testing a couple's compatibility by drawing out the details of their political views. Anyway, in our case it would not be wrong to say that soon after we were married a shared interest became the foundation for some sort of domestic harmony. Even the word 'interest' feels too strong here. To put it plainly, we both used to read personal growth books behind each other's backs. How this came out in the open and brought us closer makes for a not uninteresting story. Might as well start at the beginning, with how we met.

Like all young men I too dreamed of romancing a girl but had neither the luck nor the ability to woo one in college. When I started working, it didn't seem smart to begin a relationship with a colleague. Anyway, it's not like the women there drove me wild. I grew even more cautious after I saw the attempts of two co-workers to have some fun lead inexorably to marriage. All in all, though I was as eligible as anyone else, romance remained a distant dream. And so, when Viji's alliance came to my family through a relative, I didn't say no to a meeting. Her mother was a schoolteacher. Her father worked in a bank, this relative told us, and had preferred not to appear for the bank officer's exam to avoid the hassle of transfers. 'Very good people,' he said. 'Content with what they have. Own house in Bengaluru. Only child. Works in IT.'

At our first meeting I told her: 'I am not at all conservative. I don't believe in caste and all that. I think women are the equal of men in society.' Later, in the early years of our marriage, Viji sometimes teased me about this performance. I suppose I thought it was the kind of thing that young women who considered themselves modern liked to hear. Had I know the term then I might even have called myself a liberal.

But even without having heard that word, I had some experience of the strange satisfaction and sense of superiority that comes from denouncing caste and rituals. To be frank,

I don't know what I really believed. My attitude was shaped mostly by the instinct I mentioned earlier – about not weighing oneself down before a swimming race. Maybe it was further nurtured by the years I spent living in a hostel or the friends I made there. Those who leave their home towns and move elsewhere are always more eager to fit in. Something my colleague Hemant said one day over lunch struck me as true: 'You got a job without any difficulty. If you had experienced the humiliation of being unemployed, you may have gone to people of your own caste for help. At the very least, you would have prayed.'

After I started working, it was as if everyone at office was competing with the West, trying to outdo each other in showing off how modern they were. They behaved as if caste did not exist in society. They spoke from the most benevolent and liberal-minded positions. They seemed to believe that speaking English well was all it took to be a good leader. The easiest way to climb the ladder was to learn to imitate them. Unlike now, nobody back then had the courage to show up at office with a religious mark on their forehead.

Viji and I met a few times before our engagement. We told our families we needed more time to get to know each other and decide on marriage. This made us think we were doing something revolutionary, and we rehashed it endlessly in our conversations, thrilling at the idea that this marriage was entirely our doing. We refused to call it an arranged marriage. 'Only the meeting was arranged, the rest is ours,' became our refrain. Recently, while talking to Rekha about combining old ways with the new, I brought up our marriage as an example. Rekha, trying unsuccessfully to control her laughter, silenced

me by saying, 'Appa, I'm not a child any more. How is marrying
within the caste some kind of radical act?'

The truth was that we had liked each other right from
the first meeting. Or so I thought. I had read somewhere that
addressing people by shortened versions of their names was
a sign of affection. I called her 'Viji' the next time we met.
When she did not object, I rejoiced at the thought that she
too was fond of me. Soon it became clear that no one called
her anything other than Viji. She had been Viji for as long as
she could remember. There had even been occasions at school,
she told me later, when a teacher had read out Vijaya from
the attendance register and she had not recognized her own
name. Rekha had made fun of me several times for continuing
to call her Viji: 'You could have called her Jaya. Or you could
have turned it round and called her Jivi. You could have called
her anything but you chose the same name used by thousands
of people. Shame on you!' Viji would listen to Rekha with a
smile and then find herself at the receiving end: 'You are no
better, Amma. You call him Venkat like you are his colleague.
So boring.'

Without admitting that we liked each other, we spent six
months dithering, luxuriating in the feeling that we were in
charge of our own lives. Sometimes Viji said things that made
me think she was not someone I could control easily. For
instance, she refused to tell me her salary. 'I haven't even told
my parents. You don't have to tell me yours; I won't tell you
mine,' she said.

I don't know what changed her mind, but she told me what
it was the next day. It was a little less than mine. On such
occasions I thought she might escape my grasp if she was not

quickly tied down by marriage. I was unlikely to find someone much better when it came to looks, education and family, and there was the added attraction of her being employed. After all, a float under both arms makes it twice as easy to swim.

My family had no reason to reject the proposal. My aunt from Sagar cautioned: 'Don't go for someone too educated. Working women don't listen to their husbands.' We made this a joke among friends and relatives. When this aunt came to the wedding, I whispered in Viji's ear: 'She's the one who said you won't listen to your husband.' When we bent down to touch her feet, she blessed us warmly: 'Fight all you want, but stay together.' Reminiscing about this much later, Viji said, laughing, 'What a practical blessing! And her warning came true after all. Where do I listen to you?'

At the time young couples were beginning to prefer Kodaikanal over Ooty as a honeymoon destination. We decided to go to Kodai and stay at Sunrise, a popular hotel that looked out over a valley. After spending all night on the bus, we reached the hotel at seven and checked in after a forty-five-minute wait. We slept for a while, then began to get ready to go out for breakfast and a walk. We both tried to convince the other to bathe first. In the end, I accepted defeat and got up.

I went to the bathroom, got out of my clothes and realized there was no razor in my toilet kit. I had bought one just before leaving and shoved it hastily under the clothes in my suitcase. I opened the door halfway and asked Viji to hand me the razor. 'It's below the clothes. On the right side,' I told her.

There was a certain charm to being reliant on her in these small ways. She too seemed to like it. It showed that marriage had changed something between us. The previous night on the bus I had asked her to keep my wallet in her handbag. The bus stopped somewhere in the night, and we got down sleepy-eyed to have a snack. I washed my hands afterwards and asked for her handkerchief. When it was time to pay the bill, I asked her for twenty rupees as if she controlled all my money. This pretence of being dependent on her felt sweet and satisfying.

I shaved, bathed and emerged from the bathroom in a dhoti, with a towel wrapped around my shoulders. I looked towards my suitcase and was stunned to see that a book I had hidden inside it was now lying on top: *Living in Harmony*. The cover showed two clasped hands against a light-blue background. I ran to the suitcase and, without looking at Viji, thrust the book back inside. It was not hard to imagine what had happened. Viji had found the book under my clothes while looking for the razor and had casually left it on top of the suitcase. I kept my interest in such personal growth books a secret because some of my colleagues mocked them. I had not mentioned it to Viji either. Now, I sensed that Viji was looking in my direction and worried about how to react if she took a dig at me. I turned my back to her and rummaged through the suitcase for a shirt to wear.

Viji, who had been silent until then, said, 'I'll show you a magic trick if you turn around.' I couldn't read her tone.

When I turned around, she said, 'The book you just put in your suitcase? I'm going to pull it out of my bag now.' She put her hand in her bag, held up a copy of the book and smiled.

I have often thought that this was perhaps the most significant moment in all our time together. A feeling of comfort and affection for her burst into being. Those who read such books will understand the self-doubt and shame that accompany being seen reading one of them. Now, the very thing I was embarrassed about was revealed as a virtue in her eyes.

I stared at her and the book in her hand, and said, 'Oi!' It seemed I had forgotten how to speak. Unable to think of anything else, I gave up on the shirt and went to the bathroom to comb my hair. An exuberance had taken hold of me. I cast aside the towel from my shoulders and stood carefree and bare-chested in front of the mirror. I combed my hair jauntily, using one hand to push back strands of hair between strokes of the comb. I applied Brylcreem and left the box lying carelessly in front of the mirror. The teeth of my comb were grimy, but I did not feel I had to hide it in my toilet kit.

A thin veil of unfamiliarity had remained between us even a week into our marriage. Now, it had been flung aside in an instant. We gave up all our inhibitions, from arranging our belongings neatly to not changing in front of each other.

That afternoon we were lazing about in bed, when Viji started telling me about the new project she was involved with at office. As she spoke, I said 'excellent', encouraging her to go on. The third time I said the word it struck us both that I had picked up the expression from a book, and we burst out laughing together. Fondness for her welled up within me. I traced her cheek with my finger and softly took her name. 'Mmm,' she said, though I couldn't tell if it was a sound made in acknowledgement or pleasure. For many days after we would both dissolve into laughter whenever we heard the word 'excellent'.

I said, 'It's not a coincidence that we brought along the same book and found out like this. There is a message for us here. We are only seeing a small part of the larger picture.'

She spoke in a whisper. 'Do you think god's hand is at work here?'

'It must be. But tell me, why didn't you say anything all these days?'

'Why can't that be god's work too? Maybe he wanted it revealed today with some drama. And I could also ask you the same question.'

'It's hard to explain,' I said. 'I feel as if anyone who sees me with such books will look down on me. They have helped me grow, but people seem to think they are only for those who are immature, so I don't say anything. Why did you hide it from me?'

'I didn't hide anything,' she said. 'There was no occasion to bring it up, that's all. But I know what you mean. Once when I pulled out a self-help book from my bag, my colleague Geeta snorted and gave me a look I can never forget. I ignored her, but it only takes one or two people like that to give the entire office an inferiority complex. Like they say, one man with a gun makes the whole town run.' She got up from the bed and took the chair in front of it.

'And if they've studied in one of those prestigious colleges, don't even ask! So full of themselves. It's almost like they need to look down on others. They can't not do it,' I said.

Viji laughed. 'You've put it so well.'

Her praise thrilled me. I began to enumerate the characteristics of these people. 'No one knows better than me.'

Viji joined in. 'Everything that comes from the West is holy. Branded is the best.'

I went on. 'Lack of discipline is creativity. Breaking rules is the only rule.'

'Only I am worthy. Everyone else is good for nothing.'

'Haha . . . We can only progress by destroying our culture.'

'Arre, don't go so far,' Viji said.

'How's this: all words, no work.'

'And those words must be spoken in an American accent.'

'Say French words like the French. And Kannada words like an American.'

'Onsomble. Onvolope.'

I imitated one of them by saying 'Marathalli' without the long 'a' sound or the flicked tongue at the end. I said dosa with a hard 'd'. Viji could not contain her laughter. It spread to me too, and we relayed it back and forth, without knowing why we were laughing. I glowed with the confidence that comes from making someone laugh.

* * *

That evening we aimlessly roamed the streets of Kodai. Viji was wearing a bright-red cotton sari with a green border. As we went up and down the inclines, I told her how, the year I joined work, I went to Mumbai for a week-long management course. A man named Tiwari was one of the speakers, and some of us had gathered around him in the tea break after his lecture. When I learnt his talk was based on a book called *Another World*, I asked him, stupidly, where the book was available. I don't know what he thought, but he drew a copy from his bag, placed it in my hands, said 'good luck' and left.

I started reading it that very evening. The other world of the book was the office, and it felt like every workplace problem described in it was taken from my own office. For someone like

me, who came from a village, the office had become a place of
silent dread. There were foreign clients to deal with, MBAs
who held everything from the West as sacred. I felt suffocated
without being able to say why. This book, and then others like
it, helped me. With their pages as my wings, it felt like I could
fly over everything that troubled me at work. As I immersed
myself in book after book, I found that the things I read in
them came back to me when I found myself in those situations.
I would hear them as if Tiwari were speaking to me. 'You
know,' I said to Viji. 'His voice is deep and serious, perfect for
a guru.'

I explained to Viji that Tiwari had entered my life at a
time when I was struggling even to talk to my colleagues. On
the few occasions I worked up the courage to tell them I was
feeling out of place, they looked at me kindly and brushed it
off saying, 'Don't take these things so seriously.' There was
nothing in common between me and those who had grown
up in the city. If they brought up the music of their youth
and mentioned Metallica or Judas Priest, I would simply
go quiet.

'Oh, you poor thing!' Viji said. 'You didn't know those
bands? They're not bad. But then, why should you have heard
of them . . .'

I felt a little uneasy that she knew about that kind of
music. But I also noticed that Viji paid attention to the
smallest details when I told her about my life and ended up
taking my side. I was overcome with affection. I yearned
to unburden all my secrets to her. When I sensed Viji was
willing to let me into her world, I asked, 'Which was your
first book?'

'It was called *Talk to Me*. It's about having conversations with oneself. But it will take me a long time to tell my story. It begins in childhood.'

'What's the rush? You can go on all day and all night if you want. I am here to listen.'

When Viji started, we were standing below a tree at a roadside tea shop, her face dappled by the evening sun. Her hair was in a loose bun, held in place by a large clip. Her brown lips and the marks left by long-ago acne stood out in this light. Her nose was enticingly rounded at its tip. And how sexy a slight overbite is! She only had to part her lips a fraction to look desirable. I watched mesmerized every time she took a sip of tea and her lips moved to meet the rim of the cup. The ardour of a new marriage magnifies everything. I saw her upper lip rest on the cup's rim, test the tea's temperature and then advance with a gentle quiver to take a sip. Unable to help myself, I said, 'Hand me your cup for a second.'

'Why?' she asked, puzzled.

'I'll tell you, give it to me.'

I placed my half-empty cup on the shop's counter, took her cup in my right hand, turned it around to where her lips had touched the cup's rim, took a lingering sip and said, 'Ah! So good!'

She had caught on by now and said, teasingly, 'What are you doing?'

I rolled my eyes coyly, said, 'Nothing at all,' and handed her back the cup.

Viji plunged into her story with enthusiasm. 'You won't believe it,' she said, 'but I used to talk to myself all the time as a child.' She told me how she used to come home from school

at four in the afternoon and have the house to herself until her
mother returned from work at five. During this hour she would
stand in front of her mother's dressing table mirror and talk
to herself, complete with gestures and expressions. She would
make faces, roar with laughter, abuse classmates she did not get
along with. 'You know, once, I tried to imitate the dances I had
seen in films. I even took my clothes off and tossed them here
and there,' she said, laughing.

Her mother returned early one day, heard Viji's voice and
tiptoed in to investigate. She grew alarmed when she saw Viji
talking animatedly to herself. 'Who knows what else I might
have been doing when she saw me,' Viji said. Her mother,
fearing a mental disturbance of some kind, put an end to her
spending time at home alone and enrolled her in a tuition class
after school. 'I stopped talking to myself,' Viji said. 'Much
later, I got this book as a prize for something. Just look at the
coincidence; any other book and I wouldn't have bothered
reading it.'

Her voice had grown louder in her excitement. I finished
my tea, handed the cup back to the man running the shop and
asked for another round.

Viji said, 'Just one. I'll share it with you.'

'What are you doing?' I asked, playfully.

She imitated my sing-song from a few minutes ago:
'Nothing at all.'

I told her while we waited for our tea, 'You have my consent
even if you want to walk on your hands at home. I'll have a big
mirror installed for you.'

'No need for the mirror. I have never talked to myself after
that,' she said. She began to hum a line from an old film song:

'In the mirror of your eyes . . .' She then said softly, with a teasing smile, 'But I like walking on my hands.'

I was elated that I didn't need to hide anything from her any more. I couldn't recall where I had read that the ability to be open about one's weaknesses was the foundation of a strong relationship. Though we had seen each other for six months, everything Viji had said that day was new to me. It is impossible to know which key opens the door to a heart.

I paid for the tea and we went on our way, walking downhill without any effort. Viji asked, 'What made you bring along that particular book? I didn't see it when we were packing.'

'I put it in my suitcase at the last minute,' I told her. 'Your finding it was completely by chance. I don't know if I would have had the courage to show it to you. Let's just say everything happens for the best. Why did you choose to bring this book?' I asked, entwining my fingers in hers.

'There's a relative on my mother's side who always gives books as presents. He couldn't attend the wedding, so he gave me this book in advance. I started it and then got caught up in wedding preparations.' She unclasped her fingers and held me gently by the forearm. I walked on, feeling the warmth of her presence.

'Where are your books?' I asked.

'At home. They're mostly on maths and programming. Only seven or eight are self-help. I'll bring them over after we return.' She tightened her grip.

'I can't wait to see what you have.'

'And yours? I didn't see any at home.'

'Where was the time? They're in a box below the bed. I'll get them out when we're back.'

Without realizing it we had come to the bottom of the hill. We looked around the market, had another cup of tea and tried to find some means of transport to return to the hotel. There was none. Oh well, it shouldn't be too exhausting to walk up hand in hand, we thought, and set off.

* * *

After returning to the hotel room and resting a while, I asked, 'Shall we read together?' The thought of being on the same page as her made my spine tingle. Outside, evening was turning to night.

We both got out our copies of *Living in Harmony* and sat side by side on the bed with pillows to our backs.

'Which page?' she asked.

I leaned my shoulder into hers. 'Move a little closer so I can see the page number,' I said.

'If we're going to sit so close we don't need two books,' she said.

I promptly put my book aside and nestled my head in her shoulder. The book was open at page 87. The section's title read 'Should you tell your beloved everything?'.

'Hmm. Boring. "The Firecracker of Deceit . . ."' Viji turned the page. I had liked that section, so I felt a little disappointed. But I said nothing. After a few pages, the book took up the story of an imaginary couple, Sameer and Sushma, to discuss how a healthy curiosity about each other's shortcomings can bring a couple closer. This section was titled 'Uncover the Covered Up'.

She rested the book on her chest and said softly, 'The way you drank from my cup of tea today . . . Did you think of it yourself or was it something your guru Tiwari told you?'

I found her question deeply wounding. When I had recovered somewhat, I said, 'What do you take me for? Do you think I need to read a book to lose my temper or to love someone? Want me to show you what I can do?'

I playfully rubbed my elbow against her side to show that I was not bothered by her question. It touched her bare skin below the hem of her blouse, and she broke out in gooseflesh. I had found a sensitive part of her body to explore, and I was eager to demonstrate that I could be spontaneous. I repeated, 'Want me to show you?'

'What?' she said softly, stretching the word out.

I did not have the patience to put into words all that the question brought forth in my imagination. I pressed my cheek against her shoulder. 'You'll soon know what,' I said. 'Let's do what the book says. Uncover the covered up.'

She said 'what' again, even more softly, even more drawn out. It drove me wild. 'Uncover . . .' I whispered and with a finger touched the edge of her sari where it ran over her chest. Her hand shot up by reflex to stop me but relented after a moment. The end of her sari was caught between her back and the pillow, and I released it gently. She closed her eyes. I saw her chest, now covered only by her blouse, and the thought that I could do anything I wanted with her made my heart pound. She slid forward bit by bit, in no rush, till she was lying on her back, her arms by her side.

'I'm going to uncover everything. There should be nothing between us.'

'My eyes are closed,' she said.

I started with her ornaments. First, her toe rings. Then her anklets. Then, one by one, her bangles. It was difficult to remove them without causing her pain. I gently pressed her wrist and palm to coax the bangles along, then squeezed her knuckles and fingers to get them off. We lost ourselves in this new type of touch. I could not tell if her little cries were of pain or gratification.

Her hands were soon bare. It was then the turn of her earrings. This was a far more delicate task – the slightest touch on her ears tickled her. I took the earrings off and kept them on the bedside table. She removed her nose ring herself, replaced its screw and placed it in my hand, all without opening her eyes.

Her ring came off easily, and then I fumbled about her neck, trying to take off her mangalsutra. She stopped me with an 'un-hunh'. I was not sure what she meant, so I drew back to look at her. She looked different with bare arms, with no ornaments in her nose or ears. I needed her to be completely naked and moved my hands again to the mangalsutra round her neck.

'No, don't take it off,' she said.

'Why?' I asked. 'There should be nothing between us. Just you and me.'

'Chee, stop it. Wearing a mangalsutra is a woman's privilege. It's not to be removed once the husband ties it during the wedding. That would be inauspicious for the husband.'

With those words, at that moment, an urge to dominate that had for a long time been looking for a way to surface, emerged from the depths and began to flow in the space between us. I was now more casual in the way I went about taking off her clothes, carelessly forceful in the way I yanked at the blouse stuck to her arms.

When I was three-fourths done, she said faintly, 'The light.'

'How does it matter when your eyes are closed?'

'I'll open my eyes in the dark.'

I turned off the light. The room went completely dark. As my eyes adjusted to the little light entering the room through the window, I began to vaguely see the outlines of objects in the room.

I took off her hairclip last and tossed it into the darkness. It fell somewhere with a faint sound.

I took off the only piece of jewellery I was wearing – my ring.

I could not contain myself any longer. She reciprocated with the same fervour, her little cries and whimpers the only sound in the room. With her on all fours, I entered her from behind, the foam mattress bouncing under our weight and the force of my movement. The mangalsutra hanging from her bare neck swung gently, its pendant glinting occasionally in the faint light from the window. I was all the more enamoured with her for not wanting to take off the mangalsutra. The more I noticed the swaying of the black beads I had tied round her neck with my own hands, the more it resembled an animal's reins and drove me to a frenzy. There is nothing as exhilarating as taking possession, establishing authority. I wanted this ride to last forever.

I have never tugged at the invisible reins she herself handed me that day. I know they will not slip out of my hands. There have been times though when I have wondered if they are still fastened at the other end.

I later referred to that episode of lovemaking as 'the mangalsutra's privilege', but Viji thought I was making fun of her and protested. I did not use the term again. The experience too was never reprised. It was like the tea we had earlier that day. I have sipped tea from Viji's cup any number of times since then, but it has never felt as special as the cup we shared at Kodai. These are things that happen only once. It sounds good when people say that life, like a river, moves relentlessly on. But the idea is hard to grasp. Otherwise, would I, even after my illusions were shattered, have endlessly ordered single cups of tea to our hotel room?

An incident the next day has stayed in my mind. Just before we were to leave our hotel room, she pulled out a skirt and a matching top from her bag and showed it to me. 'Arre, I've never seen you in a skirt!' I said, looking at her in astonishment.

'I have never worn one,' she said. 'But if you say yes, I'll do so today.'

In the bus to Kodai I had felt a strange joy when I handed over my wallet and submitted myself to her. Now, I was pleased she was seeking my approval. 'Of course yes! You will look different in this,' I said.

A skirt was not ideally suited for Kodai's weather. But then, protection from the elements is not the only function of clothes. Since my college days I had looked enviously at boys who kept the company of girls in Western attire. There was something about the hairstyles of these girls, the careless way they inhabited their clothes, their ease holding a beer mug, how they unabashedly lit their cigarettes and blew out the match, that gave them a breezy, rebellious air. I never pursued one of them because I knew I would be unable to handle on the inside what looked attractive from outside. Even in my fantasies I hankered for things like marriage and making someone mine forever. I was not capable of the abandon that let these girls simply enjoy the moment.

I had not thought the skirt would be so short. It barely covered her knees. The very freedom it gave her legs did not allow her to walk comfortably. Still, she insisted on wearing it all day.

* * *

The first thing we did on coming back from Kodai was bring our books together. Viji got ready early that morning, went to her parents' house and returned with a carton. We put it down in the hall. I brought my own treasure chest there and we both sat on the floor.

The smell of naphthalene filled the air when Viji opened the carton. She explained: 'I had thrown in some mothballs because I didn't know when these books would emerge again.'

'Arre,' I said. 'See, I have mothballs in my box too.'

We sat next to each other and drew out our books one by one. The first couple of books to emerge from her carton were about mathematics. I did not recognize the next few titles. As soon as I saw *Talk to Me*, I exclaimed, 'So this is the one!' She seemed pleased that I remembered.

We sat exploring our collections like children. She got up after a while to make tea. I looked over my books quickly after she had left and thought it better if Viji didn't see titles like *Don't Climb the Career Ladder, Take the Elevator* and *The Art of Introducing Yourself.* The prospect made me apprehensive in a way I couldn't quite put my finger on. I thought of my office friend Hemant who, at our wedding, had whispered in my ear, 'Make sure you take the right book on your honeymoon.' As

I arranged my books in small stacks on the floor, I concealed some of them at the bottom.

My box had a few books from my engineering days, including the half-foot thick *Introduction to Electrical Engineering* from the third semester.

'Why have you kept this?' Viji asked in surprise when she returned with the tea.

'Just in case some interviewer gets it into his head to ask about the basics. I've not opened it once in all these years, but I still haven't been able to give it away.'

I looked at her as I drank my tea. The end of her sari was tucked in unevenly at the waist. Her cup of tea was in her right hand. In her left she held a book whose blurb she was reading.

'What book is that?' I asked.

'It's a popular book on mathematics. Great fun. I read it ages ago,' she said.

There was so much about her that I had learnt only in the last few days. Overwhelmed by how close we had grown, I blurted out: 'I have told you everything. What is there to hide from you? You could tell me everything too.'

She looked taken aback by this sudden appeal. After a moment's silence, she said, 'What is there to say? I would have told you if there was something.'

'But there must be things I don't know about you.'

'Don't be silly. I can't tell you things indiscriminately simply because you don't know them. What would be the use? Even something minor like having a cup of tea with someone could be significant, but only in the right context.'

I had brought this situation upon myself. It is difficult to be told by your wife that yes, she has secrets, but no, she will not share them with you. She said, as if she noticed me struggling inwardly, 'Let it be, don't pester me now,' and went back to the book in her hand.

To draw her back into conversation, I began telling her stories of my missteps while putting into practice what I had learnt from personal development books. There was the time I became an object of ridicule at office when I began praising my colleagues a little too obviously after reading *The Art of the Compliment*. Or the time I changed my hairstyle and grew a beard on the advice of *Change Agent*. I enacted these episodes funnily enough that she laughed and laughed and said, 'I can't take it any more.' Maybe she was overgenerous with her laughter to compensate for her sharp words. Even so, I was enthused and went on to poke more fun at my own expense. Nothing can spur on a man as much as a woman's laughter, even if it's his own wife's.

In the midst of all this, I realized that Viji hadn't looked at my books with anything nearing the interest with which she flipped through her own. An important difference between us struck me: Viji did not take these books seriously. She only read them for enjoyment, to pass time. There was no question of her trying to put into practice anything she read in them. But I believed these books could prove useful. It was not beneath me to learn something new and change myself accordingly. When Tiwari quoted lines in my ear from this book or that, I felt grateful. Hemant had said one day, 'Why do you try so hard to become someone? You're not an empty box that needs to be filled from the outside.' Sitting there among our books, a cold fear gripped me: what if she too looked at me the same way? How was I to even know what she thought?

Tiwari spoke: 'To find the depth of a dark well, throw in a stone.'

'These are all good to read but not to put into practice,' I said gravely, almost convincing myself.

'Oho, changing your views to impress the wife, Mr Change Agent?' Viji said and laughed.

'You caught me, you rascal!' I said and tried to join in the laughter.

* * *

We bought the two-bedroom apartment we now live in the year after we were married. Like all houses, ours too came with a story: it was a stroke of good fortune that we got this apartment, that too at a rate lower than anyone else and in a building constructed with the best materials. For two to three years after we bought the place we constantly repeated the account of how the person who had booked the flat had been unable to pay by the deadline, how I had happened to see the place that very day, how things had moved quickly from there on and before we knew it, as if god had bestowed this flat upon us, it was ours without our having bribed anyone or used any clout. The story was told with little sprinkles of masala like, 'You just have to look at the floor tiles to tell the quality of construction. Can you even see the join between them?'

People who visited us praised the ample storage in every room, our foresight in purchasing two parking spots and the fact that no area had been wasted in passageways. But with time, the house and the objects in it began to age. Friends and relatives bought apartments in buildings that were shinier and more impressive, that came with amenities like gyms and swimming pools. Now, the chief virtue of our apartment is its resale value in an area like ours. Over time, its glorious past has transformed into possibilities for future income.

Rekha was born two years into our marriage. Marriage, our own house and then the arrival of Rekha, all in quick succession, had some friends congratulating us on our perfect planning. 'Nothing like that,' we would say smiling, even as we accepted their compliments.

We had not discussed having kids, but one Sunday afternoon when we were having sex, I got up for a condom and she said, 'Come back, it's fine.'

'What if something happens?' I asked.

'Let it happen.'

'It's you who will bear the consequence,' I said.

'Why don't you try?'

'Everything is a joke to you. Shall I get it?'

'It's okay, don't bother.'

All this talk put us somewhat out of the mood, but we went on nevertheless. The consequence I had warned about made itself known that very month. In the days that followed I said 'It's okay, don't bother' several times to her in a funny voice, reminding her that the decision had been hers.

After Rekha was born, my mother kept saying to relatives, 'Boy or girl, it's all the same to us.' In the same tone she said, 'An older sister is good for keeping her brother under control,' making it clear she hoped for a male child in the future. I once responded, 'Putti is both son and daughter to us,' and was reprimanded by Viji: 'Why, isn't it enough for her to be just our daughter?'

Rekha's birth turned our day-to-day life upside down. When I suggested to Viji that we get a cook to ease her load, she was firmly set against it: 'My mother managed without a cook, why can't I? No one sticks around, so the food's taste keeps changing. They can't cook without pouring a litre of oil into everything – bad for health and a waste of money. And after an outsider starts cooking, I won't be able to find a thing in my own kitchen.' Despite this, I would bring up the idea every now and then. 'All you make is tea. Why don't you learn to cook something and help me?' she would ask. I would say: 'It's because I can't cook that I am suggesting we hire someone.' And so it carried on.

It was during this time that we began to understand what family life really meant. Rekha would throw tantrums over the smallest things. Both Viji and I were constantly frustrated. Then, staying at home for a whole year affected Viji's career. When she resumed going to office her workload continued to increase, but that was all the career growth she saw. When there was an opportunity to go abroad for three months, she declined. Even if we hired an ayah, it would have been difficult for me to take care of Rekha without Viji. 'Go, we'll manage somehow,' I told her, but I did not insist. In the end it was her decision not to go. This seemed natural enough, so I didn't dwell on it. Before we got married, my spine would tingle when I heard people refer to a working couple as a double-engine vehicle. But our own double-engine had begun to sputter. My career was not going particularly well. But even if I didn't rise to the top in terms of position, my salary saw regular increments and we managed to pull on without too much of a struggle.

My parents died in this period – first my mother and then, after a year, my father.

When Rekha began school, we let out a sigh of relief. We didn't know then that the troubles of family life never go away entirely. They leave only to return in a different form.

3

The next day was a Sunday, so though it was eleven in the morning, I was sitting in the hall in my pyjamas, looking at a credit card statement on my laptop. We went out for lunch every Sunday, which meant Viji had no kitchen work. She was reading the newspaper. Why must a shop's name always show up as something else in the bill, I was muttering to myself, when there was the sound of knocking on the front door. I looked at Viji and said, 'It must be them again.'

'Shall I check?' Viji asked. I motioned to her to remain where she was and got up.

I opened the door and there they were. RK was still in the blue shirt he was wearing the previous day. MP3 was in a brown T-shirt. 'Did she call?' RK asked.

I lost my temper. 'I told you just last evening that I'll let her know if she calls. What did you say your names were? MP3 or something?'

'It's a little urgent.'

'What urgent? Urgent for whom? She hasn't told us about any project, nor have we asked. Please don't trouble us any more.' I felt Viji was right when she had said their visit was not about college work. I wondered if I should try and get more out of them, but that would mean inviting them in, so I said nothing.

It was RK doing the talking this time too. 'It's not only the project,' he said. 'There's another problem.'

'What problem?'

'Our uncles have come with us. They're waiting downstairs. They'll tell you everything,' he said. Without waiting for my response, he turned to MP3 and said, 'Let's bring them.' They both went thudding down the stairs.

I came back bewildered, leaving the door open. Viji too looked surprised. There was no doubt that Rekha had managed to get herself mixed up in something. I waited with a knot in my stomach. When no one came up over the next few minutes, I shut the door, kept my laptop on the dining table and went around tidying the room. I changed into a shirt and trousers. 'Let's first find out what this is all about,' Viji said. I nodded.

The door of the lift rattled shut outside. Footsteps. Someone knocked. I got up, grumbling: 'Are these people allergic to doorbells?' More knocking before I could reach the door.

Two men appeared with RK and MP3. RK introduced the man at the head of the party: 'Our uncle.'

The man said, 'I am Raja. This is Nanda, he's with me.' They both joined their palms in namastes. Raja was wearing a half-sleeved white shirt that hung down from his paunch.

The outline of his vest was clearly visible through the fabric of the shirt. White trousers, shiny black sandals and a gold chain around his thick neck. He had short hair with the odd touch of grey. His face was clean shaven and set in an artificial smile. He looked exactly like a small-time politician from a commercial film.

Nanda was a heftier fellow in a black shirt. I noticed he had tiny boils on his neck. Five or six brightly coloured threads were tied around his right wrist.

'What is the matter?' I asked, without moving away from the door.

With his smile fixed on his face, Raja indicated with his hand that they wanted to enter. I had no choice but to step aside. The boys looked ready to follow them in, but Raja sent them away.

Raja and Nanda slipped off their footwear outside the door and came in. A strong smell of perfume suffused the air. I closed the door. They both brought their palms together again when they saw Viji. Raja took the sofa. Nanda sat beside him. Before settling down, Raja handed Nanda a small bag he was carrying. Their body language clearly showed that Raja's status was the higher of the two.

Viji folded the newspaper she was reading, got up and went inside. I wondered if it was better for her to be present, but I knew she would be listening anyway.

As I sat down on the chair opposite them, Raja began: 'Finished breakfast?'

'Yes.'

'Today is a holiday, so you must have eaten late?'

'Yes.' I gave him a look that urged him to get on with it.

'Look here, sir, I don't know if you're aware of the situation. Initially I thought it was just college kids having fun, so I let it be. Now it is getting out of hand, so we came straight here.'

His Kannada was a strange mix of several dialects. It was impossible to tell which region he came from.

My chest pounded as I waited to hear what he had to say. Then I thought I might as well strike first and launched into a complaint: 'Your boys came yesterday. I told them my daughter is away in the village. They have come again today. I kept quiet because they are classmates. Otherwise I would have shouted at them and sent them off.'

'Actually, the real problem is something else.'

'What is it then? Tell me.'

'I'll come to it, I'll come to it,' he said. 'See, our Manju, your daughter's classmate, is a little simple-minded. Weak in studies also. Soft by nature on top of that. Your daughter seems to have helped him with some college work, and now he has become dependent on her. Of course, at this age these things are bound to happen. It is when they don't happen that we should worry. Anyway, that is not the real problem.' The unchanging fake smile stayed on his face through everything he said.

'I see,' I said. I did not want to appear overeager to get to the matter.

'Do you know whose son Manju is? He is Ranganna's son, sir. That's right, Reporter Ranganna.'

The name sounded vaguely familiar. 'Who is he? What publication does he work for?'

Nanda, who had until then been signalling his agreement and deference using only facial expressions, slid to the edge of the sofa in shock at my ignorance: 'What are you saying, sir? He rules this area. One glance from him and people will pour out of every house in support.'

I must not have looked sufficiently impressed. Unable to control his emotion, Nanda began to crack his knuckles. Raja motioned to Nanda to keep quiet. He sat murmuring to himself, apparently unable to come to terms with the fact that someone could ask who Ranganna was.

From what little he had spoken so far it was evident that Raja was a shrewd man. His fixed smile and odd little movements gave the impression he was straining to contain the crookedness in him. His hands lay motionless in his lap when he spoke, as if he had to hold himself in check.

'You must have heard of the weekly paper *U-Reporter*?' Raja began. 'He runs it. U stands for Underworld. When there's a murder, he knows about it even before the police. Ranganna's influence goes all the way to the heavens. He's connected to the editor of every newspaper in the state, no matter how small or large. He can take care of a land dispute not just in Bengaluru, but in the most remote corner of the state. It doesn't matter which party is in power. When Ranganna says something, that's it. Forget corporators, even MLAs don't dare cross a line he has drawn. He doesn't take a step without a gunman by his side. We work for him.'

Raja looked at me intently, surmised that his eulogy had made its mark, and continued: 'When a man like this has enemies, does it not mean that he's doing good work? There is this fellow called Chicken Chandru. He wants to control our area, so he organized an attack on Ranganna. No one should grasp at what is beyond their reach. Are we all sitting on our hands here? Anyway, let me now come to the actual problem. Chandru's gang has a boy named Chetan. He goes to the same college. They call him Cheetah. He has threatened to thrash Manju if he is ever seen with your daughter.'

It took me a couple of minutes to process this convoluted story. It was sinking in that these people came from a world as frightening and repugnant as it was bizarre. I began to feel uneasy.

Nanda broke the silence. He said, 'His paper prints murder scene photographs in full colour. Tell me which other publication has the guts?'

I recalled seeing tabloids with gory photographs on their front pages hanging on display outside small shops. I had never actually read one of them.

Nanda leaned forward and said in a low voice, 'We would have finished off that dog Cheetah, but we didn't want to get our hands dirty.' It sounded like a movie dialogue. Even so, his words made me uncomfortable.

I feigned courage and said, 'All right. So what now?'

'So nothing,' Raja said. 'Manju called your daughter, and when he found that her phone was switched off, he came crying to us.'

Nanda said, his voice heavy with contempt, 'Actually it's his own fault. He whimpers instead of behaving like a man.'

Raja went on: 'Because her phone is switched off, Cheetah will think he has won. Manju is now depressed because she has listened to Cheetah.'

Maybe the situation was not so dire after all. Even so, I wondered if this could really be the entire story. I reassured them: 'Nothing like that, don't worry. As I told the boys yesterday there is no mobile network in the village. It's only possible to talk to her if she calls.'

Raja began to speak, 'I understand . . .' but was interrupted by Nanda, who burst out: 'That dog Chetan! Isn't it wrong for him to put conditions on a girl from our area?'

'It's a college,' I said. 'Students come there from different areas. No one should be telling anyone else what to do.' I was confident I had the upper hand when it came to talking about the ethics of the situation, but reasoned argument was unlikely to get far with Nanda.

Nanda introduced a fresh angle. 'It's only so that sister is not inconvenienced.'

'Then just leave her alone.'

'We want to, but why is Chetan not leaving her alone? He has gone and put this worm in her head now.'

'He can release a tiger if he wants. I'm here to look after her.'

'It's not like that. All we're asking you to do is support our area.'

'What does our area have to do with this?'

'Sir, don't we all take pride in our area?'

'Yes, of course. But these are not children any more. It's their choice whom to talk to and whom to avoid. No one should be scared of anyone,' I said, trying to be placatory. Their talk of areas had made me apprehensive. I had read that gangs divided up cities among themselves and fought like dogs over territory.

Raja said, 'That is exactly what we are saying. Your daughter, our sister, should not stop talking to Manju just because that bastard told her not to. That is all we want. Boss has told us to look after Manju. Doesn't matter whose body has to hit the floor, we will look after him.'

I was taken aback by the resolve in Raja's voice. Now that the guru had crossed the line and used the word 'bastard', the disciple went further and used a stronger expletive. 'Don't be scared. We will support you. Who is that *madarchod* to say anything . . .'

'Wait,' I said. 'What if she doesn't want to talk to him?'

'She won't feel like that. Sister and Manju are already friends. This has happened only because that swine has come between them,' Nanda said.

'Children fight and make up all the time. Why make an issue of it? These are silly things,' I said.

Raja spread his arms on either side so that he took up most of the sofa. Looking at his attire I thought again about how these people stayed faithful in every respect to their portrayal in films, down to the heartlessness required to commit the brutal acts shown in them. It struck me that I had not noticed if he was wearing rings. I looked at his hands and was not disappointed. Fat rings on three fingers of his right hand. He was drumming his fingers softly on the sofa, almost as if he was asking Nanda to go on.

'Don't call it silly,' Nanda continued, his voice growing louder with agitation. 'Self-respect is self-respect. Doesn't matter if the insult is big or small. He has thrown down a challenge. Now we must teach that madarchod a lesson. He's going after a sister from our area only because he wants to start a fight. He knows we will hit back. That Chicken Chandru . . . he used to run a poultry shop. One day he got into an argument with a customer and by chance swung his cleaver. That's how he went to jail and became a rowdy sheeter. The bastard

doesn't have two proper murders to his name, hardly controls
two hundred votes, but just listen to him talk! He starts some
mischief like this every now and then.'

Raja said, in a low voice, 'Look, Chandru's people are
bound to approach you. Just tell them we are supporting you.
Let's see what they can do.'

'All this is between college kids after all,' I said. 'Let us not
interfere too much.'

'But we are talking about girls, sir,' Nanda said, with the
tone of one making a particularly subtle point.

'So?'

'When it is about the safety of girls it is our duty to interfere.
You should go to the police and file a complaint that sister is
being harassed by Cheetah. Give a copy to the principal. We
will take care of the rest.'

'But I don't even know who this Cheetah is.'

'We know what a *bhenchod* he is. Trust us,' Nanda said.

He was convincing in his own way. The thought entered
my mind that Smooth Nanda might be a fitting name for
him, but it felt altogether too gentle. I had read that it was
the police who had started using epithets to distinguish
between members of the underworld with the same names.
Over time, it became a source of pride, like the titles attached
to the names of kings and noblemen. While the names were
amusing to come across in a newspaper, the same reports
detailed the horrific violence these people were capable of.
Nanda, who had surely stabbed at least a handful of people in
his career, must already have a title of his own. Had we met
in a desolate place, he might have finished me off by now.

I felt my stomach lurch. It was best to end the conversation quickly and send them away.

I said, 'Why go so far as to file a complaint? Let me talk to her first before doing anything.'

'Talk to her if you want. Sister will say the same thing we are saying. Can we call her right now, sir?' Nanda asked.

'No. As I said, there's no network in the village. Let's wait.'

'No one has a phone there?'

'It's not like in the city.'

'Okay, it's up to you. We will wait. If you file a police complaint, add that it is forbidden in your caste for boys and girls to roam around together. Then we can get him for offending religious sentiments too. Remember, Ranganna controls thousands of votes.'

I did not understand. I said, 'It's a small matter of a girl not talking to a boy. What is the connection with votes?'

'Who can say no to a bundle of votes? You are strong when you have votes, that's why I mentioned it. And we can't simply say it's a small matter and do nothing. Or it will go beyond our control. It's like a tug of war – you relax your grip for a moment and before you know it the rope is gone.' Nanda acted out this last bit about losing the rope.

Raja leaned forward and said softly, 'You don't understand all this. This is a serious matter only. We would have started a caste riot and taken care of him ourselves, but the bastard is from our caste. Same sub-caste too, madarchod.'

Viji went from the bedroom to the kitchen, glancing at the three of us in the hall. We fell silent.

Raja stood up in the manner of one who has concluded business and is ready to leave. 'Just give us a signal and leave the rest to us,' he said.

I didn't ask for his phone number, nor did I give him mine. Then it struck me that he had not asked for my number because he already had it. I was to give him a signal apparently. He hadn't even told me how to do so. The audacity of the man!

After the two left, Viji rushed into the hall. 'She hasn't got stuck in some mess, no?' she asked with some fear in her voice.

'If it's what they say, it doesn't seem very serious. We can't be sure until we speak to her. Why did you go in when they arrived?'

'I took one look and realized they wouldn't speak freely if I was here. You saw how they stopped talking when I came out. It's scary how they have inserted themselves into this whole business. Who knows what anything they say means. They didn't even seem to know Rekha's name. Kept calling her daughter and sister. Chee . . .'

'It's not like that, Viji.'

'Then what? He was sitting right here insisting that Rekha should not stop talking to Manju. Who is he to say so? And you just sat there listening.'

'Why are you taking it out on me? I didn't agree with anything they said.'

'I would have come out and kicked you if you had. It's unbearable. Three men sitting around, talking about what the women of a house can or cannot do.'

'It's not like that. You heard what I said.'

'Stop saying it's not like that! You are only concerned because your daughter is involved. You would have no problem if it was some other young woman they were doing this to. I don't know who you are sometimes. It's like there's another man inside you, waiting to get out.'

I could not tell if this was said in the heat of the moment, or if she really thought I was two-faced. Such veiled attacks on my character had increased over the last couple of months. But then, it was also true that my mind had been on edge and prone to over-examining anything to do with loyalty or trust.

I tried to act as if everything was normal, but the whole situation had left me at a loss. I said, 'I'll make some tea,' and removed myself from her presence. I had to steady myself.

Viji was deep in thought when I came from the kitchen with two cups of tea. She took a sip and said, 'If it is what they say, then Rekha doesn't seem too bothered by it. But this MP3 is a little strange. He shouldn't get overly sentimental and do something rash, that's all.' She seemed calmer.

'Has Rekha said anything to you?' I asked.

'No. This is the first I am hearing of these people,' Viji said.

'We can't imagine the world these people come from. They wouldn't think twice about slitting someone's throat.'

Viji said, as if she hadn't heard me, '*Thoo*. The whole house smells of their perfume.' She tucked her legs under her and sat more comfortably on the chair.

'She's just something for them to fight over, that's all. It will go away when their quarrel is resolved.'

'Why has that boy's father's gang become involved? Boys normally keep these things hidden. And all that talk of caste! See how their minds work. Should we go to the police?'

I had thought of this too. I said, 'We'll have to give a
written complaint if we go to the police. What will we say?
Nothing is clear.'

'Okay. But instead of keeping it to ourselves let's inform at
least one other person. How about the retired colonel on the
second floor?' Viji was fond of him.

I pretended to be unperturbed and tried to say something
light: 'Him? Your boyfriend? Hmm. What if he complicates
the situation further? Let's think about it.'

'Get a copy of *U-Reporter* tomorrow. Let's see what it is.'
She picked up the empty cups. 'I'll make some more tea,' she
said and went to the kitchen.

4

'This is all because of that school.'

Viji has expressed this opinion hundreds of times. I have stopped reacting to it. Because when I do say something the conversation quickly jumps from one thing to another and soon we are arguing about dangerous and uncomfortable matters such as class, equality, feminism and so on. It is a territory full of landmines, especially in the gaps between words and actions. I know from experience that it is impossible to return in one piece after going there.

Viji's mother worked in the office of a convent school near their house. This was the school Viji went to. Were it not so far away, we would have enrolled Rekha there without thinking twice, but since we had to look for another school, we ended up deliberating the matter. Viji wanted Rekha to study in a school similar to hers. I was keen that she go to an elite, prestigious school. Those who go to such schools are set for life simply

because of the social circle they develop there. It took me a
while to realize that every argument I made in favour of one of
these schools was perceived by Viji as an attack on the school
she went to and where her mother still worked. In the end we
applied to both kinds of schools. As if to prevent a showdown
between us, Rekha was accepted only by one of the schools
I had in mind. While this had the effect of reducing Viji's
opposition somewhat, she continued to seize every opportunity
to complain about the school.

They had parent–teacher meetings once every three months
where the discussion revolved more around the failings of the
parents rather than the children's performance. After which
parents had to endure presentations about how they could
ensure their child's development. It would not be wrong to say
that just the wealth and status of some of the other parents made
me feel the fees we paid was worth it. Somewhere deep inside
was the thrilling thought that Rekha would, over the course of
time, be absorbed into this class, that this leap upwards that
was unattainable for me might be hers. But this was a hope I
could not share even with Viji.

Before parents went off to the respective classrooms, the
school hosted a common reception. For about twenty minutes
the parents and teachers mingled over coffee, biscuits and fruit
juice. When Rekha was in the fourth standard, I met Prakash
at one of these gatherings. He came forward and introduced
himself: 'Hi, I'm Prakash. Sita's father.'

Though I didn't recall the name Sita, I knew from previous
parent–teacher meetings that his child was in Rekha's class,
and I tried to be polite. 'Oh yes,' I said. 'Our Rekha has
mentioned her.'

'Oh, you're Rekha's father! Sita couldn't stop talking about how Rekha climbed a tree on their last class excursion. Where did she learn to do that?'

'I am from Malnad, and we have an orchard in our village,' I explained. 'It's where Rekha spends her vacations. That's the source of all her mischief.'

'I suspected something like that. Otherwise where can kids learn such skills in a city? Most schools don't even have playgrounds.'

Though I was pleased he had appreciative things to say about Rekha, it bothered me that he only mentioned her tree climbing. I tried to steer the conversation in a different direction. I said, 'She's bright at studies too. Always gets good marks.'

'Oh, kids shouldn't study so much in the fourth standard,' he said. 'In fact, I was planning to raise the issue in today's meeting. At this age they should be left free to play. Our whole approach to education is flawed.'

To hear Prakash speak one might think he had been forced to admit his daughter to this school. I didn't want to listen to more of his wisdom. I changed the subject. 'Where do you work?'

He mentioned the name of a large consumer goods firm. When I asked him what he did there, he said, 'I run it.' I wasn't sure I heard this correctly, so I said nothing. The moment's silence gave two others who had been hovering about us a chance to start talking to Prakash. When they began playing the networking game of finding out which friends and acquaintances they had in common, I realized there was little chance of resuming my conversation with him and went in search of Rekha's class teacher.

I went to work directly from the school. It was only when I
returned home in the evening that it struck me that the person
I had spoken to in the morning was the well-known CEO
Prakash Khanapure. I cringed inwardly at having made a fool
of myself. I had asked many people until then what they did at
their company. No one had ever said 'I run it'. Prakash's answer
cast a spell over me for several days. When Tiwari reminded me
it was not money alone that prevented people from moving up
in social class, I realized I had illustrated the point perfectly with
my behaviour. In retrospect, the deferential body language and
simpering smiles of the people around Prakash that day made
perfect sense. I went over the incident so many times with Viji
that she grew exasperated and said, 'Enough, don't overdo it.
Every company has a CEO. There are thousands of companies.'

Rekha's birthday came about a month after this episode. I
saw to it that she invited Sita home. I expected Sita's parents
would make an appearance either while dropping her to the
party or while picking her up. Should the need arise, I had
quietly thought of a few topics that could be discussed with
someone at the CEO level.

Sita arrived at the party right on time. She had come alone.
The driver who dropped her at our doorstep said he would be
back to collect her at seven. I hoped Prakash would make an
appearance at least then, but he did not. Sita got up and left
as soon as she heard that the driver had arrived. 'Look at her
discipline,' I said, but no one paid any attention.

Later, whenever I tried to get Rekha to invite Sita over
on some pretext or the other, Rekha flatly refused. 'I don't
like her,' she said. The friendship that might have sprung up
between us never got a chance. Tiwari's reproaches for missing

such an opportunity made themselves heard for months. Even then, I found ways to slip into conversations at office or among friends that Khanapure's daughter was Rekha's classmate.

The next year Sita transferred to an even more prestigious school. It was known for not having examinations or homework. Rekha and her classmates burned with envy. No matter how high you chase such people, they create an invisible level for themselves that's even higher.

Maybe there was some truth to Viji's complaints about the school. As the years passed, Rekha turned increasingly headstrong, flighty and extravagant. Had we sent her to an ordinary school, her time would have been occupied running to tuitions and preparing for examinations. Ideas like independent thinking and liberal values are all fine in the abstract, but when your child begins to rebel at home, they turn into hot ghee in the mouth – too good to spit out, too painful to swallow.

Rebellion! What had only been a word to me began to make its meaning felt when Rekha was fifteen. The harder we tried to keep her in check, the more she defied us. There was a battle at home every day. An endless string of episodes comes to mind when I think of that phase. Why not begin with her name itself – she sulked that it was too plain. She threatened to change it to Jennifer or Isabella after she turned eighteen. Names are not owned by any religion, she argued. I tried to reassure her by saying that Rekha had been a modern name when she was born. One day, in a moment of weakness, I blurted out: 'It's the name of a film star. She was at the peak of her career when we were in college. Very beautiful.'

Rekha was aghast. 'Disgusting,' she said. 'How could you even think of naming me after an actor? Someone else's name . . . it feels so second-hand. Was she the woman of your dreams? Chee!'

'Really?' Viji said. 'You thought of naming her Rekha after the actress? I had no idea.' With Viji having washed her hands off the matter, I became solely responsible for Rekha's name. After that, I was on my own whenever Rekha brought up the subject.

It feels like Rekha grew up in the blink of an eye. I can still hear the way she used to laugh with abandon when she was not yet two years old. Her laughter would reach uncontrollable heights when we played *gaja-bhuja-bala*. The words were from my school days, and were meant to invoke the might of an elephant. Whenever we needed to push something as a group, rather than saying something like 'one-two-three', we would say 'gaja-bhuja-bala', straining in unison at 'bala'. Years later, it turned into a game at home. I would lie on the bed and Rekha, sweetly saying gaja-bhuja-bala in her baby talk, would push me. I pretended to roll over and fall from the bed, which made her break into peals of laughter, thrilled at her own enormous strength. But then, she came to think gaja-bhuja-bala were magic words that moved all objects and would try to push a chair or a table. When she was unsuccessful, she would come to me, ready to burst into tears. And then, lest she lose faith in the mantra I had myself taught her, I would apply a hand, without her knowledge, to whatever she was trying to push. These scenes are fresh in my mind, as if they happened only yesterday.

Though we grumbled about the school, we couldn't identify what exactly we had a problem with. More than anything, it was Rekha's unpredictability that baffled me. I told myself that independent thinking was essential for her personality to develop and made my half-hearted peace with it. I considered buying books on how to handle teenagers, but then thought of the scene that would ensue at home if Rekha found them and gave up the idea.

Once, when Rekha was in the twelfth standard, she insisted on going to a music concert. A few organizations had opposed the concert citing drug use in such events, and it had become a topic of discussion in the newspapers. I did not want her to go, but she was adamant. We had a fierce tug-of-war over it on the Saturday of the concert. Viji conveniently refused to take sides.

'You're worried without reason after reading the newspapers. It's not really like that,' Rekha said.

I brought up a different aspect: 'It's a waste of money too. Two thousand for the ticket.'

'You don't have to pay for it. Amma will.'

'No, she won't.'

'That's up to her. It's her money.'

'No. It's up to me.'

Viji remained quiet. Rekha said, 'I know how to get a pass without paying.' She picked up her phone in a huff and began to text someone.

'Don't make this only about the money,' I said.

'What else then? You're keeping me tied up here for no good reason.'

'Such a large crowd. Who knows when it will end at night. It's not a safe place for girls.'

'I'm not going alone! There will be plenty of friends with me.'

'You don't understand, Putti. It's not like that.'

In her rage she stomped to the cabinet in the hall, pulled out my copy of *Fight Smarter* and flung it on the ground in front of me so hard that a puff of dust escaped from it.

She said, 'It's not like this, it's not like that. You don't know what it is yourself. Read this book properly before you start a fight again.' She went to her room and banged the door shut behind her.

Viji and I were astonished. We had not expected such an outburst. Worse, it was clear that it had been building up for a while, waiting for the right moment to emerge. Knowing this sharpened the insult I felt.

After waiting a while, Viji tried to placate me: 'Let it be this time. Anyway she's not going alone.'

I said, 'I have already said no. She must listen to me.' Just then, the door to Rekha's room flew open and she emerged wearing jeans, a tight T-shirt and pale pink shoes. I put myself between her and the front door.

'Let me go,' she said, furious.

'Don't make a scene now. Ask for anything else you want.'

'I don't want anything else. I'm getting late. Let me go.'

'No means no.'

She tried to step around me, but I blocked her and caught hold of her wrist. 'Don't touch me,' she screamed. I did not relax my grip. In an instant she twisted her arm free and shoved me with such force that I would have fallen backwards if not for the dining table. Rekha realized what she had done. She said 'sorry' as she slammed the front door and rushed out.

I didn't know how to come to terms with this defeat, that too before my wife's eyes. It had felt like some sort of karate manoeuvre – the way Rekha pushed down my elbow and tugged free her arm. She had been so quick that the places where she had touched me while freeing herself were only now beginning to make themselves known by a slight burning sensation. The table corner had hit bone through the flesh of my buttocks. It did not escape me that my limp, middle-aged grasp was no match for the strength of this well-built young woman. I also knew that my hold over her was not based on physical strength alone. There was another source of power, the one that could tell Viji she was not to give her any money. But Rekha had managed to break that hold too.

Viji went to Rekha's room without saying anything. I could faintly hear her speaking on the phone. My hand was trembling slightly and my tail bone was throbbing with pain.

Rekha returned after a short while. I went to her room after ten minutes, placed two thousand rupees on the table and said, 'Go.'

She said, 'Thanks, Amma has already given me the money.' She pushed the notes back towards me.

Her twelfth standard went by while I agonized that she had yanked the reins out of my hands. My preference had been for her to do science in her eleventh and twelfth, and then go on to study engineering. But such desires must be sown early in children. Or parents must behave all along as if their preferred path is inevitable. We had not done any of this. Rekha took up arts. Then she wanted a scooter to get around. After that we lost all control over where she went and what she did.

* * *

In college Rekha developed a great admiration for her English teacher, Surendran. Whatever the subject of discussion at home, she would find a way to connect it to something he had said. No teacher of hers had ever influenced her so deeply. Viji even asked her one day, 'Don't they teach anything other than English at your college?' This Surendran was a short, thin man with bristly hair that radiated in all directions from his head. Among the things that made him popular with students was his habit of slipping out through the college back gate to smoke cigarettes. I began to criticize all smokers so I could ridicule him indirectly. I suppose I was trying to show that my contempt for Surendran was not without reason. This was a strange kind of envy. Or fear. Or something. Along with the feeling that Rekha was escaping my orbit was the restlessness brought about by her infatuation with the words and ideas of this fool.

It was certainly not without reason that I thought he was behind all the lofty revolutionary talk coming from Rekha. The books he recommended and the subjects he discussed were the kind that whipped up a storm in young people's minds. I had to become even more broad-minded to counter his influence. We started talking at home about things like patriarchy, the myth of sexual purity, the shackles of marriage and so on. There is nothing more frightening than the prospect of one's children, especially girls, coming under the sway of outsiders.

Once I found out from a photo in the newspaper that Rekha had been at some sort of women's rally the previous day. Rekha and another girl were holding either end of a big banner and marching at the head of a group of women. Even as I was trying to decide if I should reprimand her, I found out that the other girl was the daughter of the well-known businesswoman Sheela Wadhwani. This came as a pleasant surprise.

That day, in office, I made it a point to mention at lunchtime that the girl in the photo next to Rekha was none other than Wadhwani's daughter. An older colleague named Patil later drew me aside. He said, 'Idealism is a bed of thorns for people like us. It makes a peaceful life impossible. Maybe it's necessary in small amounts, but it must be kept on a leash. Children don't understand this and get carried away. I tell you this from personal experience. My son's life was ruined because he didn't know when to let go. The only jobs he can get now won't pay the rent for a small room. Half his life has gone by in dealing with false police cases.' Patil's plight and concern touched me. His words troubled me for the rest of the day. But I could not bring myself to repeat them to Viji. I said nothing to Rekha either.

A thought had entered my mind when Patil was speaking: Rekha's friend was no ordinary person. It wouldn't take more than a snap of the fingers for a friend of Wadhwani's daughter to be hired at their biotech company. Rekha may have dismissed Sita with a curt 'I don't like her', but this friendship she had formed was not a bad one at all. If protest marches could create such opportunities, then why not take them? But the occasion never arose for me to ask just how close they both were.

The three of us tried to find our respective places in the shifting balances at home. Rekha of course flew her flag of rebellion openly, but I came to suspect she had Viji's tacit support. One episode in particular left me greatly disturbed. The storm was raised by Rekha's friend Sasha.

On that night I woke up on hearing a noise. Viji was
not beside me. The bedroom door was ajar, and a whispered
conversation was going on outside. I got up and went to the
hall to find a girl sitting there.

Rekha introduced us. 'This is my friend Sasha.'

The girl said, 'Hello uncle.' They stopped talking after I
entered the room.

'So, is it morning already, or have you not slept yet?' I
joked. No one laughed.

'Sorry, Appa,' Rekha said. 'You go to sleep. Sasha will stay
here tonight.' Viji nodded in agreement.

I went back to the bedroom. I could hear snatches of their
low conversation through the partially open door. I thought I
heard Surendran's name come up, but I could not tell if I was
imagining it. I remembered having gone to bed after saying
good night to Viji and Rekha. I had turned off the light in the
hall myself. No one comes home at this hour without being in
some sort of trouble. But Viji had gone to talk to her alone,
without waking me up. I waited for her to return to bed. I
had many questions. Why was this girl here at this time of the
night? What was Rekha's role in the matter?

I only got up in the morning when Viji woke me. The first
thing I did was ask her about the girl.

'Oh, it's a long story. I'll tell you later. But nothing serious.
She was upset with something at home, that's all.'

'Do her parents know she came here? Where does she stay?'

'I'm not sure what her parents know or where she lives.
She'll take care of herself, don't worry.'

'How old is she?'

'Older than Rekha.'

'If she's not eighteen yet and her parents file a police complaint, it will be a criminal case.'

'Appa! She's twenty-two okay? Please talk softly, both of you. She's sleeping in the next room.' Rekha had entered our room.

I said, 'I don't recall you having a classmate named Shasa.'

'Sasha, not Shasa,' she said. 'You don't have to be classmates to be friends.'

'Be careful, both of you. Don't miss college today.'

'Don't worry, I'll wake her up soon.'

'Amma doesn't want to tell me what the matter is. How about you tell me.'

'Oh, it's a long story. I'll tell you later.'

'Exactly the words your mother used. You must have picked it up from her. What it really means is that neither of you is ever going to say anything. Fine, I'll ask Shasa herself.' I was beginning to lose my temper.

'Appa, please. It's Sasha.'

'Sorry. Not a name that flows off the tongue.'

'Still better than my name.'

'You've turned eighteen. Change it if you want.'

'I don't have the time.'

'Coming here in the middle of the night . . . shouldn't you be more careful? Helping someone is okay, but not if you get into trouble yourself.'

'She called at eleven and asked to stay the night. Was I supposed to say no?'

'The girl leaves home in the middle of the night. And here are you two supporting her.'

Viji said in a low voice, 'Her family forced her to marry someone a week ago. Rich families on both sides. She was in love with someone else. Yesterday she ran away and went to him. She told him she had not let her husband touch her, but the heartless fellow refused to believe her and asked why any man would possibly leave his new wife alone. She didn't know where to go, so she came here.'

I was appalled. 'Why are the two of you getting involved in this mess? If something untoward happens, it will be on our heads.'

Viji said, 'Right now, she needs our help. Are you angry because we didn't ask you first?'

'Look here, do you realize the consequences of a woman not coming home at night? Without anyone knowing where she is? Instead of counselling her and sending her home, you're bent upon ruining her life. Our duty now is to inform her family.' I was shaking in my agitation.

'If they were so concerned, they would have called by now,' Rekha said.

I did not want to argue with Rekha. I began getting ready for office. Sasha was gone by the time I returned in the evening. I tried to find out what happened after I left, but both mother and daughter would say nothing.

* * *

After that day there was a change in the way conflicts at home expressed themselves. Neither Viji nor I had the appetite for endless confrontation. At the same time making an effort to get along was like covering burning embers with ash – every compromise was another fistful of ash, but the fire inside burnt on. Of late, when we have disagreements over Rekha, I get the feeling that Viji is scraping off the layers on top to check what is underneath.

When I look back, it is hard to identify when exactly our life as a couple turned into a matter of discharging our respective duties. Perhaps it was when Rekha was born. Nothing else tests the idea of parity between husband and wife more severely. Rekha was a difficult baby. She would cry all night, ask for milk, then refuse to drink it and scream some more. Sleep was impossible at night for Viji. What little sleep she managed during the day was insufficient. Her mother stayed with us for only a month after Rekha was born. I took a week's leave and couldn't ask for any more because I was assigned to an important project. Since I was hostage to project deadlines and it was difficult to sleep with the baby's racket, I began to shut myself off in another room at night. When I would wake up in the morning and enter the kitchen for tea, I would find Viji there with puffy eyes trying to keep the household on track.

If I tried to cheer her up or say something appreciative, she found it insincere and grew annoyed: 'Enough of your drama. What do men know about having another life depend on you for twenty-four hours of the day?' Whatever she said at times like this, I would hear an unsaid, 'It's not as simple as dropping pearls of wisdom lifted from a book.' On one occasion, when she was particularly frustrated, she said, 'This house and baby are solely my responsibility. Satisfied now?'

One morning, she exploded when I suggested, for the hundredth time, that we look for a cook. She said, 'I'll drop dead working in the kitchen, but I won't allow anyone else inside. Why, are you sick of my cooking? Too bad. That's what you'll get in this house.'

I said, 'Don't be angry. Think about it calmly. Identify the obstacles in your path and . . .'

Before I could finish, she burst out: 'Enough! Please ask your Tiwari to shut up. The only obstacle in my path is Rekha. What do you want me to do?'

My pride was wounded. I considered using her own words to crush her – 'It's okay, don't bother'. Then I thought this would be too cruel and remained silent.

As Rekha has grown up, it has become increasingly hard to keep her under control. She comes and goes as she likes. Since she's never lagged behind in her studies we can't use that as a pretext to rein her in. She always has an excuse or explanation. Her friends sometimes turn up after eight in the evening and call her out. I end up staying awake until she returns. Once she came home at two in the morning. I flew into a rage that day. Viji provoked me further by distancing herself from everything. 'It's between you and your daughter,' she said.

It was a Saturday. Rekha had gone to a high-school friend's house saying it was her birthday. She left at five in the evening and sent a message at nine: 'I'll spend the night here and return tomorrow.'

I saw it after half an hour. 'No. Come home.'

'Why?'

'Don't argue. Come home.'

'Her house is very far. All my friends are here. Not safe to come alone.'

'Give me the address. I will pick you up.'

'I'll ask if someone can drop me.'

'Ready to leave. Give me the address.'

'No, it's fine. A girl here is dropping me. We'll have dinner and leave.'

'Okay. Message when you leave.'

When it was eleven and I had received no message from her, I called her phone. She didn't pick up. I messaged her again: 'Have you left?'

'So many friends spending the night. Why so strict? Have stayed with friends earlier.'

'We don't know these people. Leave now.'

'Still waiting for dinner. Will leave after eating. Go to sleep.'

'I will wait.'

'Fine, don't sleep.'

There was no message from her for another hour. I sent her another message: 'Have you left?'

'Leaving now without eating. No dinner yet. She just cut cake.'

I sat in the hall and killed time until she returned. She arrived, sarcastically said, 'Look, I'm back,' and went to her room in a huff. I sniffed the air in her wake for any suspicious smells.

While Rekha was always a difficult child, over time it became hard to tell if it was she or we making a big deal of trivial issues. Of late she has begun to attribute some of my opinions to my being a man.

Rekha grew fond of going to the village for her vacations every year, which gave us an opportunity to catch our breath. Though Viji did not like to send her there, I am sure she, like me, appreciated the respite. This time too Viji had agreed reluctantly when Rekha had asked to go to the village after finishing the first term of her final year.

Our village, Mavinamane, is in a remote corner of Malnad. The house in which I was born and raised, built two generations ago, still stands there. To get there you turn off the tar road and proceed three miles along a dirt track. Maybe half a mile less if you take the shortcut through fields and plantations. Ours is the only house for two miles. There is no one within shouting distance other than the family of workers that stays on our land. The closest market town is six miles away. The school is two miles away.

The family's land in Mavinamane is looked after by Antanna, my father's younger brother. Anyone who sees him once is unlikely to forget him because of the coin-sized bump in the middle of his forehead. Otherwise he's of medium height, slim but strongly built. Antanna has always been proficient at farm work and up for any task, including digging and hauling mud. When he was young, he could clamber up a tall coconut tree with about as much ease as he walked on flat land. He has a reputation for being stern and short-tempered. His eyes, which bulge a little, give him an added degree of fierceness.

There is no landline in Mavinamane. No mobile network reaches the area either. Last year, Rekha discovered that it was possible to connect to a mobile network by standing on a hillock about a mile away. She began going there every few days to call Viji. Now and then I receive a call from Antanna, who rings me from Raja Rao's grocery shop when he goes to the market. He has refused to buy a mobile despite my urging. 'Just another headache,' he told me. 'It's like grafting another limb on to one's body. Who will phone me here? Anyway there's no signal at the house. If required there's always the phone at Raja Rao's shop.'

There is also Raja Rao's house, only three miles away through the fields. If something urgent comes up, it is enough to inform him, and he will send a servant to deliver the message. Maybe one of the attractions of the village for Rekha is that she cannot be reached easily.

My father had to take charge of the family's land at a young age. He and his brother realized that dividing it between them would hardly leave enough for cultivation, so they stayed together. Antanna has no children. There is talk that his short temper had a part to play in his wife's death. Fearing his reaction, she apparently kept quiet about a lump in her breast until it was too late. Antanna took her to the town hospital, but only he knows what the doctors said and what medicines they prescribed. She took to bed after returning and never got up.

Antanna would wake up before everyone else at home to fire the bathroom boiler. The women were up soon afterwards. Antanna could not tolerate the women of the house sleeping longer than usual. If that happened he banged down the lid of the boiler or carelessly yanked out firewood from a stack or made the kitchen vessels clatter or slammed the back door or somehow made a noise to wake them up. Though he never said anything directly to Amma, he found ways to rebuke his wife that would prick her too. After his wife died, he began directing his anger towards the changing times and a world in which everything was going to the dogs. That world gave him more than enough opportunity to complain about women.

I don't understand to this day how Antanna, with all his boldness and aggression, could be submissive towards my mild-mannered father. If it was only because my father was older, I

am amazed at the invisible hold the institution of the family
has. Or maybe I have misjudged my father's personality. He
seldom did anything himself when his younger brother could
do it for him. This included disciplining me, as a result of
which I was more scared of Antanna than I was of my father.
Antanna would smack me hard on the back or arm when I
least expected it – punishment for a mistake taken note of a
day or two ago. It was this that kept me afraid of him. He
would hit me and say, 'Tell me what this is for.' I would have
to search my mind for a transgression in the recent past. Such
interrogation would sometimes extract from me misdeeds that
Antanna didn't even know about. Those would be punished
separately. He raised his hand on me until I was in the tenth
standard. Then he stopped as if a button had been pressed
somewhere. Viji detected an imperious note in his voice the
very first time she met him. More than that, she noticed that
I shrank imperceptibly in front of him. She didn't particularly
like him, which was part of the reason she didn't want Rekha
to go to the village.

It was Antanna who had lovingly taught Rekha to climb
trees. He revealed a tender side when he was with her that I
had never seen before. I remember Rekha as a child, tailing him
everywhere as he went about supervising work on the plantation.
Until she was ten Rekha made a big fuss whenever it was time
to leave the village for Bengaluru, insisting she would stay there.
Viji would fume silently at Antanna for encouraging her. One
of Antanna's nicknames for her was 'boss' – everything would
be hers one day anyway. And as if that nod to her authority was
not enough, he even had 'Rekha Farms' painted on a post near
the gate.

The only woman left in the house after my parents' death was the cook Bayakka. Viji was uncomfortable with the idea of a young girl spending weeks on end in a house without women. I would remind her of Bayakka's presence and try to reassure her.

Viji had heard some loose talk about Antanna and Bayakka. 'Aiyo, she's an old woman,' I had told her, to which Viji had laughed and said, 'She's an old woman *now*.' No one knew the truth of the matter, and though rumours had swirled for a long time, they didn't bother anyone. Antanna's business was his own. He has declared that he plans to stay on in the village until his death, and so there will always be a mat in that house for Bayakka to sleep on.

All through my childhood I was troubled by the thought that there was a secret in our family that I did not know. It was born of witnessing occasional fights between my parents, from hushed discussions between the three elders at home. I also felt that this ghost that wandered through the house from time to time had something to do with my mother's younger brother, Ramana. As I grew up, I pieced together fragments and reached an understanding of what it was.

Amma's parental home was in Hitlakai. Her father was among the influential people of the village, and he owned four acres of thriving plantation land there. Appa too had four acres of land in Mavinamane. The year after my parents were married, Amma's family was on its way to attend a wedding somewhere when the boat in which they were crossing a river capsized. Her parents died, but her brother, the eleven-year-old Ramana, survived. My father and Antanna shrewdly decided that Ramana would stay at our house and brought him to Mavinamane before other relations began to eye the property in Hitlakai. They sold the land and house within a year and used the proceeds to buy four acres of land next to the tank in our village. Appa declared in front of the panchayat and relatives from Ramana's father's side of the family that this land belonged to Ramana and he would act as custodian until the boy was old enough to manage his affairs. The truth was that Appa had bought the land in his own name. Amma did not realize this for over a year. When she asked him about it, Appa had the ready excuse that Ramana was a minor and the land would be transferred to him when he came of age. Amma emphasized at every opportunity she got that the land was her younger brother's by right. She referred to it as the Hitlakai plantation. Appa and Antanna called it the plantation near the tank. Once Appa said, 'It doesn't matter what we call it. It will remain as it is, where it is.' To which Amma said, 'Then let's call it the Hitlakai plantation.' Appa taunted her: 'Call it what you want. It will continue to be in my name.' On this subject, Amma was willing to confront anyone. And by anyone I mostly mean the two men of the house.

I have a strong recollection of something that happened when I was around eleven. Some distant relatives visited us and left. They had barely crossed the gate on their way out when Appa pounced on Amma, shouting, 'Hitlakai, Hitlakai all the time. Better watch out if you bring it up in front of visitors again. You are trying to set your side of the family against me.'

'Didn't you make a promise in public? What is wrong in talking about it?'

'How dare you talk back to me? Am I not raising your brother? Without me he would have been an orphan on the street.'

'That costs nothing compared to what his land produces.'

'Oho, does the prince work there with his own hands?'

'He's eighteen now. Transfer the land to him.'

'Let him come here and say he will live in the village. I will make the land over to him the same day.'

'Is this your new excuse?'

Right then, Antanna began to rage at his wife in the kitchen, who had inadvertently spilled a vessel of water. He turned it into an unforgivable crime and shouted at a pitch that increased by the second. Of course, the target of his fury was not his wife alone. He could not say anything directly to his older brother's wife, so his tirade was meant as a warning to both women of the house.

'Slipped from her hand she says. What else will happen if you sit around getting fat like this?'

' . . . '

'Didn't I tell you to shut up? So good at talking back. You all need to be shown your place. If we keep carrying you on our heads like this, you'll only shit on us.'

' . . . '

'What fortune did you bring from your parents' house that you're so proud?'

' . . . '

'Talking talking all the time. Your mouth would have splintered by now if it had been made of wood. You won't stop this nonsense without a few tight slaps.'

Antanna's fury did not abate until Amma stopped talking
and went to the backyard. That day it seemed as if Appa had
outsourced even the control of his wife to his younger brother.

Relatives from my mother's side used to visit Ramana from
time to time. This might have been a strategic move on Amma's
part to ensure there was no funny business about the land.
Ramana had always been interested in studies, and it was Appa
and Antanna who encouraged him and made arrangements for
him to study in the town. This might have been their counter-
strategy. Of course, this is all conjecture on my part. My earliest
memories of Ramana are of him returning to the village for his
vacations. Ramana was already studying in the town by the
time I began school.

For several years, Amma's anxiety that her brother might
be swindled left her with no peace of mind. And then, she was
tortured by the guilt that instead of fulfilling her obligation to
her parental home, she had allowed what rightfully belonged to
it to be taken over by others. It is only now that I can clearly see
the situation she was in, unable to trust her own husband. At
the time they seemed like trivial fights between a couple. Just
like the demon in the story who kept his life in a parrot's body,
Amma's life resided in that plot of land near the tank. Appa
knew this and from time to time tightened his grip on this
particular parrot to make it squawk. He only had to remind her
the land continued to be in his name for her to agonize over
letting her own family down.

After having seen her husband's deviousness, it must have
been unbearable to live with him, to serve him. And what
exacting service it was: from his snuffbox to his tumbler of coffee,
from his dhoti to his towel, everything had to be brought to

him. And don't even ask if something he was eating or drinking went down the wrong way. He would have a fit of high-pitched coughing, expectorating in between as if he were retching up his intestines. 'Look at the ceiling, look at the lizard,' Amma would beg, and he would turn up his teary eyes and dripping nose to gaze blankly at the roof. The sounds he made were so fearsome it seemed impossible they could originate in a human body. After a few minutes, after the cough was under control and Amma had wiped his nose and mouth, he would resume eating. Sometimes he managed to have a coughing fit even while swallowing his own saliva, so this terrible scene occurred at least twice a week. Once, I remember, he had a coughing fit while eating at a wedding and called out for Amma. The sight of her rushing to help him in spite of her bad knee is imprinted on my mind. When I got married, Amma was relieved that the wedding concluded without him having an incident. Amma began to suffer from knee pain when she was barely middle-aged. The relentless work at home made it worse by the day. Had her knees received a fraction of the attention that Appa's coughing fits got, she would not have spent her last days bedridden, unable to walk.

I have not told Viji about many such details trapped in the crevices of my childhood. Revisiting them feels like taking a stroll near a dormant volcano. Not just that, revealing too much would only be giving her a stick to beat me with. Whatever justifications my father and Antanna presented, the ignominy of having usurped a wife's parental property hangs over our house. We have smeared ourselves with the ink of betrayal. I have not told anyone about overhearing someone say at a family function: 'Steal an arecanut or steal an elephant, you're still a thief. Might as well steal the elephant.' Matters like this become known to both sides at a wedding as if by magic. I have no doubt it reached Viji's family in full detail. What must they have thought of us? What did they have to consider or overlook or forgive before agreeing to this marriage? Viji has never opened the door to this corner of her mind even in our closest moments together. Nor have I been bold enough to knock.

5

Despite trying my best to push them out of my mind, my Sunday was preoccupied with thoughts of Raja and Nanda. I felt as if something from beyond my horizon was knocking on the door to be let in. I knew Viji was disturbed too though she was putting on a brave face. It was the first time people like them had entered our house. They had sat where our guests usually sit. Every small detail about them reinforced my preconceptions – from Raja's expressions to the shape of his nostrils, from how he sat to the way he spoke. Nanda had sneezed into his cupped palms and wiped them on the thighs of his trousers.

It was hard to accept there were aspects of Rekha's world that lay beyond my comprehension. I believed that the precociousness she had shown in other areas was unlikely to extend to matters of love and sex. When I expressed this to Viji, she said, 'That is the hope of a man who is her father.' Viji and I had been caught up in an unstated competition to show who understood our daughter better, who was closer to her, more concerned for her well-being. In the process we had been needlessly lax when it came to laying down clear rules.

We both woke up later than usual on Monday morning. Over tea I said to Viji, 'I will call Raja Rao and send a message asking her to call back.' My mind would not be at ease until I had spoken to her about the boys and their uncles. 'He won't be able to convey the message before tonight. She will only call tomorrow.'

Viji said, 'Say it's urgent. He will send someone immediately. This must be the only house on the planet that can't be reached by phone in this day and age.' Her anger and frustration were evident.

While getting ready for office I went to the balcony, leaned over the railing and looked at the gate and road outside. A steady stream of people was passing by. I had to use only a little imagination to see Raja and Nanda's goons among them. I came in quickly and closed the balcony door.

* * *

I rang Viji as soon as I got off the phone with Antanna, at around five that afternoon. She didn't pick up but sent a message: 'Will call in half an hour if not urgent.'

I replied: 'Very urgent. About Rekha. Call immediately.' I waited a few minutes for her call, and when it didn't come, I called her again.

'What?' she whispered. She must have been in a meeting.

'Did you see my message?' I asked.

'No. Tell me quickly.'

'Antanna just called. He says Rekha left for Bengaluru on Saturday evening.'

'What are you saying? Did you hear him correctly? One minute . . .' Even over the phone I could hear a tremble in her voice. I heard her say 'Excuse me' to the people she was with. 'What did he say? Tell me clearly,' she said, her voice now louder. She must have left the room in which the meeting was going on.

'I heard him correctly and made him repeat everything. Come home right away.'

'What did he say? Tell me again.'

'I called Raja Rao in the morning and told him Rekha was to get in touch with us immediately. Antanna came to the town and called me. He said she left on Saturday evening. He dropped her to the bus stand himself.'

'Oh god! I'm leaving now. Did you try calling her mobile?'

'Switched off. I'm on my way home. We'll talk there.'

I reached home and sat on the sofa, waiting for Viji to arrive.

Five minutes later I heard the lift door open, followed by Viji's hurried footsteps. She unlocked the door in a rush and entered. She shut the door behind her, threw her handbag and the bag with her lunch box on a chair, and in her distress began firing a hundred questions at me. The force with which she had flung her lunch bag caused an uneaten orange to roll out. She said anxiously, 'Where did she go? If she left on Saturday she should have been here yesterday.' Choking up, she said, 'What happened to our baby?' and began to sob.

I didn't know how to share her distress and said things I didn't entirely believe myself: 'Where will she go, she will definitely come home. Let's be positive.'

'Just let her come home. She's never going to that wretched village again.'

'This has nothing to do with the village, Viji,' I said.

'Why don't you go and rot there.'

The room was quiet except for her occasional sniffling. As the silence grew more uncomfortable, I picked up the orange from the floor, took out her lunch box from her bag and went to the kitchen to put it in the sink.

'Why are you going after that lunch box? Think of what we can do. Do something. Please,' she screamed at me, her voice quivering.

It was not clear how I should shoulder the responsibility. I came to the hall and sat next to her on the sofa. It troubled me to see Viji panicking. I would have to be strong here, there was no other way. Viji was sitting next to me with her face lowered into her palms. I placed a hand on her back to console her, but she sprang up at my touch and sat in the chair opposite. I was not sure if this reaction was connected to the words we had just exchanged, or if it was part of the general hostility she had of late been directing towards me.

I said, 'Antanna will talk to Suresh and call again. You know who I mean – the guy who runs that *Sidinudi* magazine. He was at the bus stand, so Antanna came home without waiting for the bus to leave. He may have some information. Let us not assume the worst.'

'Forget all that nonsense about positive thinking. We need to do something. She's left for home and not reached. What positive thoughts can we have?'

She was attacking any target that presented itself. I did not answer and she continued to sob quietly.

After a while, I asked, 'Should we go to the police?'

'We should first talk to those boys,' Viji said. 'They came on Saturday evening too. You should have taken their phone numbers. Where do we look for them now?'

'Do you have the phone numbers of any of her friends? Maybe one of them will have MP3's number.' I started going through the contacts on my phone. I found nothing useful other than the number for her college.

'What's his name? Yes, Reporter Ranganna. If we track down someone close to him we might get MP3's number. We *will* get MP3's number.' Viji was thinking clearly again.

'We can reach Ranganna by inquiring at an auto garage or one of those small cigarette shops,' I said.

Viji flared up. 'Garage it seems. Do you think this is a movie? Don't be stupid.'

I grew angry at her calling me stupid. I said hotly, 'No, it is such people who have these contacts. People like us don't need them. But we must not go to them before talking to the police. And why shouldn't things happen as in the movies? Don't people imitate Hindi films and dance crazily at weddings?'

'Let's *do* something. It's not enough to sit at home and argue.'

The phone rang. 'It must be Antanna,' I said and took the call. It was. He told me about having gone to meet Suresh.

Viji interrupted from time to time, trying to imagine the other side of the conversation: 'Has she come? Where did she go? With whom?' All through I was gesturing to her to be patient.

Before the call ended I said to Antanna, 'I will leave tonight and be there tomorrow. She's a young girl. Shouldn't he be more responsible?'

I gave Viji the gist: 'Antanna thinks Suresh knows something. He was evasive and wouldn't give straight answers. He apparently told Antanna that she would definitely return by tomorrow and that we shouldn't panic and go to the police.' I was tired by the time I finished.

'The way you were talking I thought she had been found. Isn't this Suresh married?'

Viji's irrelevant question annoyed me. 'So? These newspaper fellows are turning up everywhere like bad omens.'

'I've never liked her going to that dump. Why didn't we ever think about what draws her to the village? She said she wasn't going this time, but then suddenly decided to go. She made such a big fuss when I asked her not to. What could be so urgent?'

'Let's leave for the village tonight. I'll book tickets.'

'We know she's not in the village. What will we do there? You were saying something about responsibility on the phone?'

'It seems Suresh said she's a responsible young woman who can take care of herself, and she will be back soon. He even said that Rekha could only reach Bengaluru if that was her intended destination. Antanna doesn't trust him. He asked us to come immediately.'

'So should we file a police complaint here or not?'

'We can't catch tonight's bus if we go to the police station now. Let's start our inquiries first. She was in the village after all. Better to file a complaint there if it comes to that.'

'There's a Jaishankar in my office who is related to the police commissioner. He will help if we ask.'

'Okay, maybe later. Let's go there first.'

I phoned the travel company. We got two seats in the last row of the bus. I said, 'There were only two seats left. He said we wouldn't have got anything after fifteen minutes. Luck is on our side.' She must have realized I was turning this insignificant thing into a good omen only to make her feel better. I am sure she wanted to believe it too.

It grew dark as evening set in. Neither of us had the will or energy to get up and turn on the lights. At least we had got tickets. And Antanna's phone call held out a thread of hope. When the room was almost in darkness I got up and switched on the light. Every object in the room stood out in the sudden burst of it. The newspaper lying in disarray caught my eye and I wanted to fold it, but everything else felt irrelevant in the middle of this crisis.

Viji, sitting listlessly on the sofa, took the wrinkled end of her sari into her lap and by force of habit began to smooth it out with her palm. She then realized she was doing this and stopped.

'Shall I make tea?' I asked.

'I don't want anything,' she said. 'See if you can get through to her phone.'

'I've already tried four times.'

'Try again.'

I called Rekha again. 'Same. It says switched off.'

Viji then tried the number on her phone. 'The message is in Kannada,' she said. 'That means it was switched off inside the state. This guy in my office lied about where he was, but he

got caught because the network messages were all in Marathi.'
For just a moment she drifted over to the world of her office.
'I was in a meeting when your call came. We were finalizing
a contract with a client. But what to do, I had to walk out. I
couldn't even explain. I just sent a brief message saying it was
a family emergency. I'm sick of saying thank you to people
asking if I need help. What trouble this girl has got us into.'

'I'll withdraw some money from the ATM. Better to keep
some cash,' I said and got up to go.

'Could this be a kidnapping case?'

'Don't let your imagination run wild. All I can get out of an
ATM is twenty thousand rupees. Would anyone ask just that
much for our child?' As soon as I said the words I realized the
absurdity of the conversation and stopped talking.

Who knows what was going through Viji's mind. Maybe
she thought everything I was saying or doing to deal with
this crisis was picked up from a book. I said, 'That girl who
had come here, what's her name, Shasa or Sasha, do you have
her number?'

'No. I don't have any of her friends' numbers. She doesn't
share them.'

'You let her spend the night here, but don't take her
number. What if Rekha came to Bengaluru and went to her
house?' I said, with some annoyance.

'Why bring that up now? I'll send Rekha a message. She
will see it when her phone connects to the network again,' she
said, and busied herself with her phone.

I went to Rekha's room. Her table was tidy. Viji
followed me. 'I arranged it yesterday,' she said, picking up
and replacing a few things on the table. I lingered there as

if something ordinary might show itself in a new light after what had happened.

I went out and returned with money from the ATM. We had three hours before the bus. The auto ride to the bus stand would take half an hour at most. We both half-heartedly packed some clothes. We were hungry but didn't feel like eating. I brought some rice and curd on a plate and told Viji she had to eat. She protested when I tried to serve her pickle, as if even at a time like this, a sense of normality could sneak in disguised as food. After a few morsels she said, 'I can't eat any more,' and went to the kitchen to keep her plate.

We took an autorickshaw to the bus stand. I noticed bananas dangling in a shop there and asked Viji if she wanted one. 'No,' she said. 'I can't eat. You go ahead.' While our anxiety was shared, she seemed to think we experienced them to different degrees. I went to the shop and came back with two bottles of water.

I tried to sleep on the bus despite being in the last row. Every town and village the bus passed through had at least two to three speed breakers. The driver took the front wheels of the bus over them with a care that did not last until it was the turn of the rear wheels. That the most patient bus driver cannot resist the temptation of an empty road ahead is a truth well-known to anyone who has occupied the last row in a bus. The bus would slow down a little when it approached a settlement, and more lights became visible through the windows. I took this as a signal to brace for speed breakers. The jolt of the rear wheels going over them was enough to launch a person into the air, and I had to grab the armrests to hang on. Once when I did this, my hand found Viji's by accident. She snatched it away as if a stranger had tried to hold it. I felt like I had been slapped hard. I turned and saw that her eyes were closed.

I sat looking into the darkness outside the window. This was a route I had traversed many times. Like actors in a play seen after their costumes have come off, places I knew well by daylight were unrecognizable at night.

The bus normally reaches the crossroads for the village early in the morning, around half past six. A large tank is seen here on the right side. From there it's a walk of three miles to the village along a mud road. Those who intend to get off here must exchange pleasantries with the driver, either before leaving Bengaluru or over tea at a rest stop, and request him to provide a halt.

The morning outside began to get brighter. 'Have we overshot the crossroads?' Viji asked.

'Don't you think I can tell?' I snapped.

Soon enough the bus stopped. We thanked the driver and got off. A gentle, cool breeze blew from the stand of trees by the side of the road. 'It was so hot in the bus. This is nice,' I said.

'Hmm,' Viji said non-committally. It must have felt like a betrayal of our distress to even notice something pleasant.

We walked without speaking. It was a mud road but not dusty. Plantations on either side had encroached upon it, making it narrower as we went on. I imagined Rekha walking here by herself. Usually, Antanna waited for her at the crossroads. Once or twice, when the bus had arrived early or Antanna had been late, she had set off by herself, meeting Antanna midway. Later she had taken great pleasure in recounting these exploits.

After the final bend the plantation's gate came into view. Next to it was the entrance to the house and its yard – three stout bamboo poles slotted into a pair of wooden posts. Shrubs growing along the wire fence formed a wall of green around the plantation. A path went through the front yard to the house. The backyard was full of fruit trees, and there was a banana grove to one side. In the front, the platform of an open verandah ran from one end of the house to the other, interrupted in the middle by steps leading to the main door.

As we approached the house, Viji said, 'Don't shout at Antanna. It will only create more chaos.'

'He should not have returned without seeing her safely on the bus.'

Antanna emerged from the house and welcomed us in. We took off our slippers and climbed the steps to the door.

'Have you found out anything?' I asked impatiently.

'Come in first, let's talk,' Antanna said.

The front room held four chairs and a wooden bench that ran along one of the walls. I sat on the bench. Antanna took a chair. He said, 'See if you want to freshen up. Coffee is ready.'

'All that can wait. First tell me about Rekha.' I had meant to say the words in a cutting tone, but they somehow lost their edge when said to him.

Antanna said Rekha was supposed to stay longer but changed her mind on Saturday and said she needed to leave that very evening because some college work had come up. Antanna told her it would be difficult to book a ticket at such short notice. But she was adamant, so he somehow got her a seat on that evening's bus. He sent for the sole autorickshaw in the area, driven by a man named Paddanna, and went to the bus stand with Rekha. They ran into Suresh and his wife, Kavita, there to see Kavita's aunt off, who was also going to Bengaluru.

The bus was late, and Antanna wanted to ride back in the same rickshaw, so he left after asking Suresh and Kavita to make sure Rekha got on the bus. 'It was only after you phoned that I went and spoke to Suresh. I should not have trusted him,' he said.

'What did he say?' Viji asked.

'He wasn't clear about anything. He said all kinds of things: I put her on the bus; who phoned you; it's not my fault if she got off the bus before reaching Bengaluru; is she a little girl; she can go where she wants. When I raised my voice, he said don't worry, she will be back soon. I think he's hiding something. No matter how many different ways I tried to get it out of him, he kept saying the same things.'

I stood up. 'Let's go to his house right now.'

'Okay, let's go,' Antanna said. 'If he leaves home, we can't get hold of him before evening. Paddanna's rickshaw isn't available before ten in the morning, so we'll have to walk. It's three miles by the shortcut. There's only one cycle here. Putti used to go everywhere on it, even to Suresh's house.'

I couldn't resist rebuking him. 'Why didn't you call and tell me she was leaving? Now look what has happened,' I said. Viji sat quietly.

'How are you all?' Bayakka entered with coffee for us. Viji took out a tube of toothpaste and brush from her bag and went to the bathroom. I picked up a tumbler of coffee.

Antanna, Viji and I got ready in fifteen minutes and set off through fields and orchards for Suresh's house. Along the way I asked questions and Antanna answered.

'He was a small boy when you left the village to join college. So he must be around forty now. He did his MA and then studied law. His wife, Kavita, is a nice girl – speaks affectionately, likes being with people. Rekha used to visit them all the time, and Kavita never let her go without feeding her. He got a teaching job at the college in our town. It's not like too many people want to be posted to this dump anyway. But he created some trouble there – instigated students, gave speeches, filled their heads with ideas of revolution and what not. Despite all this, they say he was a good teacher. In the end he rubbed too many people the wrong way and had to quit. He then started a weekly magazine called *Sidinudi* that he runs out of a small room in the town. He owns quite a lot of land, so he doesn't rely on the magazine for a living. Even so, the magazine is doing well, I hear. There was nothing here until now to put out local news, gossip, quarrels, affairs. Almost every house in the town subscribes to it.

'There was a big fuss some time back about a Gowda boy running off with a Brahmin girl. They say Suresh was the one who supported them. Taught them about the law, police, their rights as adults and so on. No one is sure who the two are, whether they were even students of the college. Everything is rumour and hearsay. Some people say it's a story he made up to see which side people take in a matter like this. It ran for weeks in his magazine. That was when it became popular. The couple was never identified, and no one around here has any first-hand knowledge of such an incident.

'But it's true that he writes every week about issues facing this area, about problems with government schemes. He has supporters and he has enemies. He writes "M.A. LL.B" in front of his name in the newspaper. That in itself looks like a threat. He's the first to find out when there's any trouble in one of the nearby villages. You remember the two Naxals who were shot in the forest here two to three years ago? People say they met Suresh before escaping into the forest. This is all rumour. God only knows what the truth is.'

Naxals! The mere mention was enough to send a chill down my spine. It also evoked dark memories for our family so I was surprised Antanna could utter the word so easily. I broke the spell of uneasiness that had come upon me and said, 'I don't think I know this Suresh.'

'You may have forgotten him, but you must have seen him around. He's not a bad fellow like that. But when people get high on saving the world, you never know where they see injustice. He can turn on you when you least expect it. During the last harvest, he got the workers together and put it in their heads that they should not work on the day of the festival. Our own workers felt uncomfortable going against tradition, so they came for ten minutes, paid their respects and left. This is the kind of mischief he creates. Some have asked him why he insists on setting people against those of his own caste, to which he says he belongs to no caste. Then he writes about all this in his magazine. He's made up insulting names for the politicians of the district. Everyone enjoys it as long as it is others who are being criticized. He says let them file for defamation if what I have written is false.'

The path led us to the top of a hillock. Antanna stopped for a while to catch his breath. He pointed to a tiled roof amidst trees at the end of the path leading down. 'That is Suresh's house,' he said. 'The road on the other side joins the highway. It's possible to drive up to his house in a car.'

The three of us came down the hillock and stood in front of the house. A worker was busy inside a cattle shed.

The front door to the house was open, the yard in front of it clean and well-swept. It had an air that suggested its occupants had woken up a long time ago and were now preoccupied with work. The house itself was old, with a large outer verandah and a dimly lit interior. Antanna called out Suresh's name. To the right of the main door's frame was a round, old-fashioned doorbell. I pressed it. There was no corresponding sound.

Antanna rattled the latch and called out Suresh's name again. His wife, Kavita, came to the door. She looked at us, surprised: 'Arre, how come so early in the morning, Antanna? Is everything okay? Come in, come in. He's gone for his bath. Should be out any moment.' She moved some chairs around in the front room and put away the books lying on a teapoy. The air inside was humid from all the surrounding vegetation.

Antanna, Viji and I were tired from the walk. We sat down. 'You seem to have come walking,' she said cordially.

'No chance of getting Paddanna's rickshaw at this time,' Antanna said. 'You must have recognized him? Our Venkataramana. This is Viji. They arrived by the morning bus.'

'Of course I know him. He may not know me though. It's a good thing you all came now. I was about to make some tea. I'll make some for you as well,' Kavita said with a liveliness that filled the room. She went in, emerged with a tumbler and a vessel of water, and placed them on the teapoy. 'You know when I saw you?' she said, turning to Viji. 'Several years ago. At your cousin Anagha's wedding. You had come to Shivamogga for it. And then, your Rekha is my friend. She comes here all the time.'

Kavita was so spirited that I lost myself for a moment in observing her. Her sari was hitched up so it would not get in the way while she worked, and her knees were visible. She was wearing thin, silver anklets. Her hair was tidy – she must have combed and plaited it after waking up. She wore a somewhat large bindi on her forehead. Her smile exposed tiny canines on either side. Her face was a little flushed, probably from the heat of the kitchen stove, and beads of sweat dotted her forehead. Her every little movement conveyed her exuberance. I noticed that Viji too had her eyes fixed admiringly on Kavita.

'He's just gone in to bathe,' she said. 'The pan is already on the stove. You can have a dosa each, and then when he's finished with his bath, we can have tea together.' The fragrance of the heating pan had spread through the house.

'No, no, just tea is fine. A quick word with Suresh and we'll leave,' I said, trying to stay impassive.

'Oh, but why? Have you already had breakfast?'

Antanna said sharply, 'No, we haven't eaten. This is not a good time. Nothing for us today.'

Kavita looked at us with incomprehension. She addressed me and Viji: 'You walked all the way here and now you are going to walk back on just a cup of tea? Antanna is used to it, but the two of you are not. And you're visiting our house for the first time. If you eat, Antanna might as well. Come in – the pan is already on the stove.'

There was no way to escape her hospitality. The three of us sat there for a moment without saying anything. From Kavita's manner it seemed she knew nothing about Rekha having gone missing.

'Why are you quiet? Come in,' Kavita insisted.

Viji got up first. I was tired from the walk and hungry. I surrendered and followed Viji. Antanna did not object either. We passed through a dimly lit living room to enter an immaculately tidy kitchen. Large windows and glass panes among the roof tiles ensured it was brightly lit. To one side was a dining table with six chairs. Kavita showed us the kitchen counter: 'Look, we had this done recently. Doesn't it look like a kitchen from the city?' She noticed us looking at the fridge and joked: 'Oh, we have everything. But the power goes out so often that it is only a cupboard.' Kavita set four steel plates on the table and tumblers for water.

She served chutney in our plates and kept talking as she poured out dosas on the pan. 'It's impossible to get workers here. I had to pull the husk off two coconuts myself yesterday. We have to beg someone to come when coconuts have to be brought down from the tree. And then they refuse to husk a few coconuts for our use.'

Antanna joined in with his complaints: 'Our plight is the same. The other day Shivappa went and brought some workers in a van from twelve miles away. This is like people in cities driving their cars to work. It was barely five when the van returned sounding its horn, and the workers piled in and left. How will any work get done at this rate?'

The first dosa came off the pan but wasn't served to any of us. Kavita answered our unasked question as she poured out the next one: 'Oh, the first dosa is always poured on a little thick. It's to win over the pan. Otherwise it acts up and makes you lose face in front of guests. Just watch, now the dosas will turn out thin and crisp.'

Kavita served Antanna first. She tried to give me the next one, but I directed her to Viji's plate. Viji put the first morsel in her mouth and exclaimed: 'It's so good!' Kavita lit up with happiness. 'Oh, coconut dosas always turn out well when the coconuts are good. These are from our own trees,' she said.

'I wouldn't be able to make them so well even with the same coconuts,' Viji said, flattering Kavita as she deserved.

A dosa had just appeared on my plate when Suresh entered the kitchen. He was wearing a lungi around his waist and was bare-chested, with a towel dangling from one shoulder. 'I heard voices and wondered who had come so early in the morning. Give me five minutes,' he said and hurried out of the room.

'Come fast, don't take hours,' Kavita called after him. She turned to us: 'I'll make tea now. He needs tea as soon as he comes.'

The ten or fifteen minutes we waited for Suresh felt like an eternity. We finished eating. Kavita gave us cups of tea. She sensed that Suresh was testing our patience. She said laughing, 'After all, he has to get his hair to go back in a wave just right,' and made a small combing motion with her fingers in front of her forehead. Viji and I had been immensely stressed over the last day, had spent all night on a bus and were exhausted from walking here in our desperation to learn something about Rekha's whereabouts. And yet we were sitting around eating dosas as if we were in no hurry. It all felt strangely disjointed.

'Sorry I made you wait. If I had known you were coming I would have bathed earlier and been ready,' Suresh said when he finally returned. Judging by his clothes he was heading out soon. 'I go for my bath only after the water for tea is on the stove,' he said and looked to his wife for agreement.

'He doesn't perform pooja after his bath, but there is the ritual of tea,' Kavita said, laughing, and handed Suresh his cup. No one reacted to this. 'Drink it quickly, it will get cold,' she said and turned her attention back to the pan on the stove. Their cuteness began to grate.

Suresh kept talking while he drank his tea. 'I'm leaving early today because the DC is coming to town. Is there a single project these people have not bungled? And then when we write about it they start shouting. I have fought and won four defamation cases filed against me. Seven are pending. I've got used to it now.'

Suresh was a tall, well-built man. His face was clean-shaven. He was wearing a pale-blue shirt and black trousers. His vest peeped out near his neck from under the shirt. Already drops of sweat had begun to glisten on his forehead and the tip of his nose, which was broad, with flared nostrils.

He went on: 'We have no proper moral education. That's why we are in this situation. If children are not taught early to tell right from wrong a country goes to the dogs. We should teach them to recognize filth even if it is in their own house. And then, we should teach them to throw it out.'

As Suresh spoke, I looked at his hair swept back in a wave and seethed with rage about having to wait while he had stood fussing in front of a mirror. He had not even bothered to ask us why we were there. Clearly he wanted to put off any mention of Rekha for as long as possible.

Suresh moved on to another subject – 'See, in a theocratic state . . .' – but I interrupted curtly: 'Suresh, enough of this pretence. You know why we are here. Where is Rekha?' I noticed his expression change slightly.

He spoke without hesitation: 'You have come all this way
to ask me about Rekha? I will tell you the truth. I don't know
where she is.'

'Ei, what nonsense is this? What have you done with her?'
I shouted. My hand was trembling. I stood up, unable to help
myself. My words tripped over each other as they left my
mouth. 'Come with me to the police station. Abducting young
girls, you bastard. Tell me right now where she is. Theocratic
state it seems . . . shove it up your backside.' My whole body
was shaking with anger.

This sudden explosion alarmed Kavita. 'Antanna, Antanna,'
she stammered.

Suresh remained calm. 'Sit down,' he said. 'Stop shouting.
As I told you, I really don't know. Why would I abduct her?
Wherever she has gone, she has done so of her own free will.
She's a young woman of twenty, not a little girl. You can go to
the police if you want. But in my view, it is advisable to wait
another day.'

'What is all this?' Kavita asked Suresh, her expression
betraying disbelief and fear. She had been taking care of her
guests with enthusiasm, and now, out of nowhere, there was
talk of abduction and the police.

'All this,' Antanna said, 'is the doing of your great husband.'

The way Suresh ignored our outburst and offered calm
advice convinced me that he was a seasoned hand at whatever
game was being played here. My hunch was that he knew where
Rekha was and that she was probably safe. My worry eased a
little. But only for a moment, until I thought of *U-Reporter*'s
Ranganna. I had found out more about him. Ranganath had
started out as an ordinary reporter. Then his life changed

because of the contacts he made while working on a series of articles about underworld dons. He must have realized there was a fortune to be made by knowing what to write and what to leave out. He started his own magazine and reached heights that required him to walk about flanked by gunmen. Maybe, I thought, these two reporters, Suresh and Ranganna, were connected in a previous life. Maybe they remained in touch, who knows.

'Tell me where she is,' Viji implored.

Suresh softened a little on hearing the desperation in her voice. 'I understand your concern,' he said. 'I will tell you everything I know. But you must listen to me patiently. Antanna came yesterday and started shouting without even hearing me out.'

For the first time the suspicion entered my mind that Rekha might have run off with someone. I said, 'We have raised her to be independent. We have not said no to anything she wanted. It will be the same if she likes someone and wants to get married.'

Viji immediately understood why I was saying this. She added, 'We don't care about caste and all that.'

Suresh said, 'Aiyo, she's not that kind of girl. She will do what she wants, and she will do it openly. It's nothing like that, don't worry.'

I burned from hearing him speak as though he understood Rekha completely, as if she confided everything in him.

'It was a mistake to let her near you. We should have kept you in your place.' Antanna's tone was withering.

'Antanna, please don't think I have betrayed you in any way,' Suresh said.

'She came to stay with me. I am responsible for her. If something happens to her, I won't leave you alive.'

'Are you threatening me?'

Antanna could be reckless with his words when he was angry. He said, 'It's not a threat. I will do it and show you. I trusted you, and now I am ruined. That poor girl came here for her holidays, and you have gone and shoved her into a ditch.'

Smoke rose from a dosa as it burned. Kavita rushed to the stove and lifted the pan off the flame.

'You were the last person to see her. Now come with us to the police station. This cannot wait any longer,' Antanna said sternly.

'Fine, let's go. I'll go wherever you want. But first hear what I have to say. It's your decision after that.' Suresh took his cup and gulped down the tea that had by then grown cold. His manner betrayed no urgency. 'I don't know if she has mentioned this to you, but she wants to be a journalist. She's come by my office several times and asked for a hard-hitting story to work on. This time it was she who brought the story idea and offered to report it. I was initially hesitant to send her. But then I saw her hunger and agreed. I think she's going to return with something explosive. Just watch how she makes a name for herself. She will be back by evening, don't worry.'

'Where have you sent her?' Viji asked, her voice trembling.

'I cannot answer that question. Beyond a point I too don't know the specific location. These things work on trust. But she's sure to return today.'

'What is she writing about? Tell us *something*.'

'Please wait until she is back. I can assure you that she has not gone against her will.'

What he said drained the life out of my limbs. Going by how secretive he was being, the only possibility I could think of was that he had sent her to some Naxal camp. The dreaded word was already near the top of my mind after Antanna had uttered it on our way here.

'How could you push a young girl into such a dangerous situation? God knows what ideas the poor child has in her head. She can't write four sentences in Kannada,' Viji said, her voice breaking as she spoke.

'Would I ever put her in danger? Ask Kavita if you want. Whatever language she writes in I'll publish it in Kannada.' Suresh spoke as if it was Rekha's great privilege that he had taken an interest in her. Now that her name had been mentioned, Kavita nodded stupidly in agreement.

For a moment I wondered if he had ensnared Rekha in some sort of romantic relationship. She was a girl of twenty with thoughts of rebellion and revolution. And he was a man who used words to instigate, who promised to change the world overnight. I looked at his face closely. I could see no reason for Rekha to find him attractive. I tried to flush the thought from my head.

Antanna was still fuming. 'There's no need for her to make a name by writing for your rag. All you print is gossip about family quarrels,' he said.

'You don't know what you are talking about,' Suresh said. 'I bring irregularities and corruption out into the open wherever I find them. Do you know how viral our reports are on WhatsApp? Hundreds of people call after reading them. A bad smell spreads quickly. And it lingers longer.'

'Just let her come back. I swear on my life she will never return to this village again,' Viji said.

Antanna said, his voice almost a growl, 'Now tell us where she is. We'll go and bring her.'

'I've told you, Antanna,' Suresh said in a soothing voice. 'She'll be back this evening.'

Kavita said to Suresh in a faltering voice, as if she were stunned by how this had gone on right under her nose, 'What is all this? Tell them what you know.'

Suresh was curt with her: 'You don't interfere now. Wouldn't I tell them if I knew?'

'If you don't know where she is, how can you say so confidently that she will be back today?' I asked.

'I know her well. She's tough. She will finish what she's gone to do and return.'

I did not like his implication that he was close to Rekha. I said, 'I'm not prepared to wait any longer than that, Suresh. If she's not here by evening I am dragging you to the police.'

I got up to leave. 'Wash your hands here,' Kavita said. 'We've put in a wash basin.' She led us to the back entrance of the kitchen. We washed our hands one after the other and went to the hall. Kavita had not yet regained her composure, but she did not forget to hand us a towel to wipe our hands. I could not bear to stay there any longer.

'I'm keeping an eye on you,' Antanna told Suresh, glaring at him. 'Don't think you can run away before evening.'

'What have I done that I should run away? Anyway, there's no point trying to make you understand.'

'We understand the doings of oversmart people like you very well. Your underground activities must be exposed. Let people know who you really are.'

'Underground,' Suresh repeated with a laugh. 'For people like you it's merely a word. But there are some others who try to stand up to injustice. You may wonder why I interfere in the affairs of others. But I must when it becomes necessary. I don't care what you think.'

'Save all this for your paper. Just tell us where Rekha is,' Viji urged.

He said nothing.

We stepped out. In the yard, Antanna asked him again: 'Tell us the truth. Since when have you been making use of her?'

Suresh remained silent.

'They're all used to this,' I said to him bitterly. 'As if those who don't even yield during police interrogations will answer when asked politely.'

Antanna spoke even more harshly: 'A donkey won't listen until it is thrashed. Not three and a half people read that rag and he thinks it is a world-famous magazine.'

Suresh was not provoked. He spoke calmly, praising Rekha: 'She is an extraordinary girl. She thinks differently about society, politics and relationships. You should be proud of her. It seems to run in the family. You should try reading her blog posts sometime. She is very brave. And I'll be happy if my paper does something good for even three and a half people.'

Antanna flew into a rage when Suresh mentioned our family. 'We've had only one bad seed and that too wasn't really from our family. Don't talk about things you know nothing about.'

'It all depends on how we see it, Antanna. Some people take it upon themselves to set right the injustices done by others. There are those who don't hesitate even to go against their own families.'

Antanna flared up further. He said, 'Stop talking in riddles, Suresh. Any bastard who messes with me will find out what I am capable of.'

Viji said, 'Why didn't you send your own wife?' She quoted a proverb: 'Easy to donate cattle that don't belong to you.'

Suresh replied with another proverb: 'A costume to suit the play, a horse to suit the chariot.'

I didn't want to make a scene just when we were leaving, so I held myself back. Some of the words he had used – 'politics', 'brave' – filled me with dread. 'Tell me,' I said, 'what exactly do you mean when you say she thinks differently about politics?'

'Let it be, there's no time for that now. But is there any place left today where politics hasn't entered? That filth has sneaked into the kitchen too. My own sister's husband has turned into such a fanatic that she is fed up and ready to leave him. Rubbish pours into his phone through the day, and he reads bits of it out to her and taunts her by asking "What will your brother say about this?"'

I found myself feeling anxious and short of breath every time he spoke. I had had enough. I left after saying, 'I'm telling you again. You have until evening. After that you are the first accused.'

The three of us were overcome by exhaustion within minutes of leaving. Antanna began to complain: 'That Paddanna is the laziest fellow on the planet. The sky can fall, but he won't get his rickshaw out before ten in the morning. He thinks he is doing an office job. Just wait till there is another rickshaw here. No one will bother with him. These are the kind of fellows

Suresh supports. His politics is only about making life difficult for others.'

Antanna was not done with Suresh yet. 'Thinks he's going to change the world but takes half an hour to comb his hair. All empty talk.'

We walked back home without saying much else to each other. As we crossed the gate, I couldn't help looking at the post and what was written on it.

As soon as we entered the house, Bayakka called out to Antanna: 'Shall I make coffee for everyone?'

Antanna said, 'Some tender coconut water would have been nice. But there are no workers right now. I'll have a few brought down when Aayu comes.'

Bayakka heard him from inside the house and said loudly, 'Aayu is not coming today. His wife is here at the back.'

Aayu's wife came to the front yard and stood in a corner. She murmured something to Antanna in a language he alone could understand. Then his shouting took over: 'Did he already have a fever or did he get it after I sent for him? If I were younger I would have climbed the tree myself. Honnappa lives near your house. Ask him to come. You people deserve an award for your acting.' She stood there looking bored. She must have heard the same words many times. When his ranting subsided, she said she was leaving and walked off impassively. 'Send Honnappa!' he shouted after her and entered the front room.

'Let it be, Antanna,' I said. 'I don't want a tender coconut.'

He said, 'It's not only for you. Rekha likes them and she will be back soon. There's not a single one at home. This is our village paradise – struggling with workers day in, day out.

First, we must bring them here in a royal procession. Then they have to feel like working. And your daughter complains if she hears me screaming at them. Tell me, is it possible to survive in a place like this by following the rules of the city? This is the only way I know. I have told her that she can do as she pleases when the responsibility is on her shoulders. Who is going to work here without being shouted at? I pretend to shout, and they pretend to work.'

Antanna had a long list of grievances. 'I didn't say anything in Suresh's house because we had gone there for something else. But it's people like Aayu that he goes after and spoils first. If they don't work in fields and plantations, what else do they have? It's not like I pay them poorly. All he does is set people against each other and watch the fun. Even a mouse thinks it's a lion when a few supporters shout slogans in its praise.'

Viji was lost in thought. She sat quietly holding the tumbler in which she had been served coffee. After a while, Antanna addressed both of us in the manner of someone offering sage counsel. Without looking either of us in the eye, he said, 'It's not that we are scared of anyone or anything. But the fewer the people who know, the easier it is to handle. We don't have to announce it to the world. When it comes to matters involving girls, best to keep it as quiet as possible.'

Viji went in with a frown on her face. I did not say anything. Antanna, with the air of a man making use of a break in the proceedings, walked to the backyard.

6

After lunch my eyes began to shut of their own accord. Viji looked sleepy too. Whenever we visited the village we slept in a bedroom attached to the hall. We went there to rest for a while. My head had barely touched the pillow when I smelled Rekha's familiar scent on it. She must have been using this bed. I closed my eyes but could not fall asleep no matter how hard I tried.

Viji sensed that I was awake. She said, 'I feel we should be doing something to find Rekha. But we're not because we believed Suresh when he said she would return today.'

'Let's wait until evening. If she is not back by then, I will perform Suresh's last rites myself.'

We did not speak any more. After a while it seemed like I might manage a small nap. I was completely exhausted. Words and images from the morning flitted through my mind, including Antanna's comment about supporters who shouted slogans.

That was an exhilaration I had known only once. When I was in college, the students had gone on strike, asking for better hostels and a postponement of examinations. We had boycotted classes and taken out a procession. Walking as part of a large group, at one point, I found myself in the front ranks. The boy leading the sloganeering thrust a megaphone in my hands. I initially refused but took it grudgingly after he said, 'Just five minutes. My throat is dry.' He told me to lead a chant of 'Our march is for justice'. My voice was not very strong. I feebly said into the megaphone 'Our march is . . .' and a roar behind me went '. . . for justice'. The response from hundreds of voices electrified me. I grew louder and more confident knowing I had followers behind me. My enthusiasm grew further when I shouted 'We want . . .' and heard '. . . justice' in reply. A boy next to me taught me more slogans. I marched ahead flashing the megaphone. 'One, two, three, four . . . hostel warden has to go.' I felt a kind of intoxication from this crowd that was dancing to my rhythm. As if to test my powers, I changed the line and received the correct response. After about ten minutes, someone came to take over the megaphone from me. 'Wait, just two minutes,' I said and shouted a little more.

Viji was asleep and breathing heavily. The hall and the yard outside were visible through the partially open door. The plants and trees outside, motionless in the sun, looked like they were in a photograph. A postman arrived on a bicycle and handed a letter to Antanna, who was sitting on the verandah platform. He opened the letter, glanced through it quickly, said 'Notice for our society's meeting' to no one in particular and raised his voice to exchange pleasantries with the postman, who was hard of hearing. He then came into the hall, impaled the letter on a length of wire and hung its hooked end back on a nail.

That wire was perhaps two and a half feet long and older than me. A wooden disc at its base supported a stack of letters. The wire was bent into a hook at the other end so it could hang from a nail or peg. Its end was pointed to make it easier to pierce letters with. The wire was thick enough that, despite having letters up to its neck, it carried their weight easily.

At one time Ramana's letters, their bellies pierced, hung from that very wire.

* * *

In those days, Ramana was one of the very few people from the village who went to the city for his studies. Neither Antanna nor my father had studied beyond the tenth standard. But Ramana prepared for his examinations like a man possessed and managed to get to Bengaluru. From there he went to Hyderabad and Warangal. Other than the letters he occasionally wrote to my mother, we had no contact with him. No one knew what work he was doing. But since he never asked for money, it was assumed he earned enough to take care of himself.

No matter how far back I cast my mind, I can only see Ramana in the village on one of his occasional visits during the holidays. Just as with Antanna, I had tried to call him Ramananna, but it soon turned to Ramanna and finally settled at simply Ramana. And so, though he was older than me, I addressed him by his name. As he was my maternal uncle, Amma, at one point, tried to make me call him 'Ramana mama' but that effort came too late. In any case, none of this made a difference to Ramana.

It was obvious on his visits that his heart was not in the village. He always seemed eager to leave. Despite this, he was on friendly terms with everyone without being particularly close to anyone. Sometimes he would sit near the well talking with Aayu, who worked in our plantation. I remember Antanna once summoning Aayu to ask what Ramana had told him.

Ramana saw injustice in things small and large that no one else paid attention to – from the cups in which workers were served tea to their salaries. He found fault with everything, beginning with the donations received by the school to the manure used in our plantations. This would begin two or three days after he came home. Appa and Antanna clearly disagreed, but they chose to say nothing to him directly. Instead, they muttered behind his back, saying things like, 'What does he understand. It's not like the city here.' Maybe they were trying to avoid friction in case he, in the heat of argument, brought up the land that should rightfully have been his. They both couldn't wait for him to leave.

A strange tension set in at home the week before Ramana was due to arrive. I recall having heard Amma say on many occasions: 'We must settle things this time.' Of course, this was easier said than done. Besides, I don't recall ever hearing Ramana bring up the matter.

Ramana knew how to quote the rule book to government officials and get them to behave. This made him popular in the village. His arrival brought a stream of visitors to the house who wanted him to accompany them to the taluk office to help expedite their work.

When Ramana's name came up one day, the school headmaster, Hanumanta Rao, said, half complaining and half proud, 'Strange boy. He's difficult to understand. He gets worked up over tiny things. Even the date at the corner of the blackboard must be perfectly written. He behaves as if he's a schoolmaster himself. It's difficult to go through life looking at everything through a magnifying glass.'

My mother was the one person who truly cared for Ramana. What she felt towards him was a combination of affection, responsibility and duty all tightly woven together. When he visited, she prepared the buttermilk dosas he was fond of. He liked to eat the raw dough used to make papad, so she once waited all summer for his arrival before making that year's supply and setting it out to dry.

My childhood world turned livelier when Ramana arrived. He always had something new to tell me, so I was only too happy to spend time with him. He described how astronauts had set foot on the moon before I was born, and he did so in such thrilling fashion that, years later, when I saw actual footage of the event, I was disappointed. My attraction for him began to fade as I grew older. The things that Ramana talked about changed as well. Sometimes I was puzzled by his behaviour. When I was in the ninth standard, he picked up my maths notebook, noticed the 'shri' I had written at the top of the first page and asked me, 'What does this mean?' When I said Torve-master had told us it was auspicious to begin by writing 'shri' with two vertical lines on either side, Ramana fumed: 'How can he teach mathematics while stuffing the heads of his students with superstitious nonsense?'

Ramana went to the school the next day and quarrelled with the headmaster. Torve-master, who was gentle by nature, did not dare look in my direction after that.

We had almost no contact with Ramana after he left the village. The only news we received of him was from the letters he wrote every couple of months. And these were almost impossible to read because of his handwriting. His Kannada looked like some ancient undeciphered script, as inscrutable as the writing of fate itself. More than one of Ramana's teachers at school had looked at his notebook and wondered if crows and sparrows had walked all over the pages leaving footprints. And they were astounded when he passed the board exams. One of them had gone so far as to advise him to write with his left hand, hoping it would force him to write slowly and therefore more clearly. As long as he was in school, the prospect of examinations kept his handwriting somewhat tolerable. Afterwards, it went completely to ruin. It takes a special talent to write so recklessly – maybe it needs to originate in a corresponding chaos deep within a person. And maybe it also requires the kind of contempt for the system that Ramana had.

His letters had Amma's name on the envelope. This annoyed both Appa and Antanna. 'How will anyone know who Sundari is?' they would grumble, but this never seemed to get in the way of the letter being delivered. The letters began with 'To my dear sister'. Or so we believed. Because we could not be certain about a single word in his letters. It wasn't even clear what script these knotted, twisted, winding, slithering, overwritten, crooked, jagged marks on the paper represented. Ramana was aware of this talent of his, and so he had someone else write the address. But he wrote the 'To' above the address himself in

English. Those who think it is impossible to go wrong while
writing characters involving no more than two short lines and
a small circle should see the way he destroyed them. The O
sometimes hung above the T like a noose. Or it was scrawled
below the vertical line of the T. Sometimes the two letters were
next to each other but too close making it appear as if the T had
grown a pot belly. His address, written within the letter, would
again be in English, looking like a tangle of thorny bushes.

Appa would shout 'Ramana's letter' as soon as he received it
from the postman. On several occasions, I sat on the verandah
in front of the house with Appa and tried to read the letter
as soon as it arrived. Appa's patience would run out in a few
minutes. He would give up, saying, 'Let him go to hell. Who
knows what he writes. Go keep it on the table.'

The next phase involved leaving the letter on a table below
the wall-clock in the hall. A rock served as a paperweight and
beside it was kept a fountain pen with red ink. We all looked at
the letter while passing by it in the course of the day or sat with
it when we had a few minutes to spare. If you looked at it long
enough and tried hard enough, the seemingly random marks
on paper sometimes resolved into likely words. Whenever one
of us thought we had deciphered a word, we would write it
down between the lines in tiny letters.

This process sometimes resulted in sentences that made
no sense: 'Shortage of funds is the foundation of beloved
superstition flower garland.' At times these sentences lacked
verbs and left us with no clue as to what they were trying to say.
Sometimes we used already decoded fragments to guess what
word might come next and tried to see it in Ramana's writing.
In the process it was easy to lose track of meaning. A sentence

arrived at after a long struggle might make no sense in relation
to the rest of the letter. Such sentences would then have to be
reassembled. So, though a sentence like 'I have lost my heart to
the old women of Kerala' was one that could plausibly occur
in a letter from Ramana, we knew we had gone wrong when
the next sentence read 'And so the bank people have started to
make trouble'. Or a sentence like 'It gives me great pleasure to
tell you that my wife has been ill for the last week' was unlikely
all by itself. More so since Ramana did not have a wife.

Amma would remember the words she had identified, run
them past me, saying, 'See if this fits,' and then have me write
them out. I don't recall her ever writing anything on her own. I
can still see her standing there peering at the letter and guessing
at its contents as if it would take her closer to her brother, who
could be anywhere.

It took a couple of weeks for this process to yield something
that could actually be read. This journey from strange squiggles
and marks to script, from the letters of a script to words, from
words to intelligible sentences, and finally, from sentences to
meaning, felt like a speeded up demonstration of how language
evolved in human civilization. Amma would have me write out
a reply a day or two after we had managed to make sense of a
letter. I would then put Ramana's letter on top of the other
letters on the wire and hang it from its nail on the wall.

Each of Ramana's letters had something specially for
Amma, even if it was a line like, 'The dal here takes a long
time to cook.' Every letter, after he was done with day-to-day
matters, ended with a few lines on history or politics. This
was the hardest part to decipher. It sometimes had words we
hadn't heard of before – 'bourgeois', 'tyranny'. How were

we to even guess at them? Trying to make sense of these few lines in that impossible handwriting was like squeezing water from stone. Appa had sarcastically named this part of the letter Golden Words. It typically had lines such as, 'A day will come when people will grow sick of it all. Their calls for justice will grow louder.'

Ramana himself had trouble reading his handwriting. On one of his visits to the village, Antanna thrust an old letter into his hands, pointed to a line and said, 'What have you written here? I can't make any sense of it.' The letter, full of red ink, looked like a battlefield. Ramana squinted at the line for five minutes and then said, 'Oh, now that I'm here there's no need to read this any more.'

Though no one brings it up now, the uproar caused by Ramana's last letter is etched permanently in our family's memory.

It was the beginning of June, and I was getting ready to join my engineering course in a few weeks. Appa took this as a pretext to organize a Satyanarayana puja and call friends and relatives for a festive lunch. The house was full of people and good cheer. After lunch the men sat at one end of the open verandah in front of the house chewing betelnut.

The women had gathered on mats in the verandah some distance away. Venu-mami was lying down on a bench, pretending to be deaf while listening to the conversation. Her husband, Venu, had died when she was middle-aged, and she had no option but to remain in the house of her husband's extended family, helping with chores. Her own name had long been forgotten and she was called Venu-mami after the man she had married. She quickly realized what the fate of a childless widow in a large household was. Her main strategy for self-preservation became a feigned deafness. She claimed her hearing had started to fade from the shock of her husband's death, and within a year established herself as completely deaf. To go along with it she began to shout rather than speak. Her deafness came in handy when she was erratic with her chores or spoke against the men of the house. And it came as a boon that her husband's family baulked at the expense of a hearing aid and kept postponing her appointments at the district hospital. She knew that the term 'keppi' – deaf woman – had been attached to her. 'Say what you want,' she would roar. 'Anyway I can't hear a thing.' She had grown older but had not given up her deafness. As she liked to say from time to time, 'Where does a woman's plight change with age?'

Amidst their banter, some of the women teased Venu-mami with questions and laughed at everything she said. One of the women said, 'We had gone to Tippanna Bhatta's daughter's wedding. Everyone was stunned by how grand it was. Cold drinks were served with lunch, just imagine.'

Venu-mami heard this and turned to them. 'Aiyo, why did you go there? You shouldn't take even a drop of water in Janardana's house. He's such a miser he might be keeping track of how much you drink. They're the kind of people who look for fish in their own piss.'

There was a roar of laughter at her misdirected comment. Only those who knew that Venu-mami and Janardana's family did not get along realized that her words were not as innocent as they seemed.

The attention encouraged her to continue putting on a show. 'Go on, laugh all you want. People laugh when I say it as it is. Don't think I can't hear. I can hear everything. Did I say something wrong for you all to laugh like that?'

A little girl went up to her and screamed in her ear: 'Venu-mami, is it true that you can't hear?'

'No dear, I don't want jalebi now. Had more than enough with lunch. Let's see when I have tea,' she said, indicating that she expected jalebi with her tea. This was cause for more merriment. Venu-mami was legendary for being able to drink endless cups of tea without regard to the time of day.

The men, from where they sat, were enjoying the ripples of delight emanating from the women's end of the verandah. Perhaps it was the languor born of a full stomach, but my usually stern father was in a relaxed mood too.

One of the women said, 'Sunanda's husband has been transferred to Shivamogga.' When Venu-mami did not say anything, another woman prodded her: 'Did you hear that, Venu-mami?'

Venu-mami bellowed: 'Yes, yes, I heard. They are trying to get Ramana married to our Sujata, but I will not interfere. It will happen if it is to happen. But it's a good match.'

More laughter ensued. Venu-mami had indirectly expressed her desire and it had been understood by those it was aimed at. Sujata was related to Venu-mami. When the proposal had been brought earlier, Amma had said, 'Let Ramana first agree to get married. We'll see after that.'

Someone asked, 'Who? Our crows-feet-sparrows-feet Ramana?' There was laughter again. This seemed to remind the men about Ramana.

'Big-hearted fellow. He's the only person I have seen who, when you have tea together, fights genuinely to pay the bill.'

'The people at the taluk office tremble with fear when he speaks.'

'It's been a while since we saw him here. Does he write often?'

'He writes. But the trouble is even the gods cannot read his writing.'

Then, on a whim, Antanna said, 'Do you want to see his letter?' Without waiting for a reply, he went in and brought out a letter from Ramana that had arrived a week ago. Everybody had been busy with arrangements for the puja, and we had not deciphered it yet.

One of the men in the group, Raja, took the letter from Antanna. He squinted at the marks on the paper and instead of reading 'To my dear sister', as every one of Ramana's letters started, falteringly made a series of sounds that amounted to gibberish. There was an eruption of laughter. Antanna looked pleased with himself at having thought of bringing out the letter.

A fellow named Panju said, 'All right, give me the letter. I will read it,' and came forward as if to snatch the letter from Raja, who was only too happy to hand it to him.

A glance at the letter was enough to make him realize what he had taken upon himself. He seemed stunned. A few of the women had by now begun to take interest in the letter. For a short while, Panju got lost in the puzzle in front of him and then read the salutation correctly. Then he was stuck. He looked up from the letter to see the entire group staring at him expectantly. He lost his nerve and tried to hand the letter back.

Antanna laughed. He said encouragingly, 'It's okay, move on to some other part. We can't read his letters at one go either.'

Panju raised the letter slightly as he looked over it. His attention rested on something near the bottom of the page. He was clearly stringing together shapes into words and sounds in his head. Finally, he said triumphantly: 'Sakina's kiss!'

'Excellent. Read it again, let's see,' someone said to tease him. Panju, absorbed in the letter, did not realize his leg was being pulled. 'Sakina's kisses,' he read again, loudly.

'Go on, go on. Let's see if he says where, when, how many,' another of the men said and the group erupted again.

Panju realized what was going on. 'Arre, I'm only reading what is written here,' he said. 'See here. "I find Sakina's kisses preferable . . ."' He managed to add a few more words this time.

'Does he prefer Sakina's kisses so much that he has to write to his sister about it?' one of the men said, snorting while he tried to control his laughter.

Panju went on, falteringly: 'I am not scared of Sakina's kisses.'

Everyone had something to say amidst the hilarity that greeted this line.

'Such a braveheart! Not afraid of being kissed. Wah!'

'Sakina's kiss must be quite something.'

'There Venu-mami is pushing Sujata on him. Here you are saying Sakina. This Ramana is turning out to be a player.'

'Go on, go on, don't be shy!'

'Don't keep all the fun to yourself. Read it out loud. He's not the kind of guy to stop at kissing.'

From years of experience, Appa and Antanna knew that whatever anyone thought they were seeing in the letter was only their imagination. They sat there beaming, enjoying the farce playing out.

Then a fellow named Gurudasa said, 'I used to be his classmate. I'll read the letter.' Panju promptly turned over the letter to him, as if having been Ramana's classmate obviously qualified Gurudasa for the job.

Gurudasa looked at the letter for a minute or two and began reading, slowly but coherently. He finished with the salutation and continued with the body of the letter. One of the men joked: 'Read what is in the letter. Don't make it up as you go along.'

Gurudasa said, 'Did you know the teachers at school had me read out his answer sheets? He passed his exams only because of me.' This didn't seem implausible given how easily he was reading.

'Why didn't you tell us before?' Antanna asked. 'We have been struggling all these years.'

As Panju had done, Gurudasa moved his gaze to the bottom of the page. Everyone waited to hear about Sakina. Gurudasa's expression changed to one of bewilderment. His eyes left the letter and he looked around. He seemed grim, as if the letter contained bad news of some sort. The men around him were waiting for what he had to say, ready to burst into laughter. As if it was too much for him to go alone against the tide of all the laughing, shouting and hooting, he steeled himself and spoke. He said the words quickly, like unleashing a fierce beast into an innocent crowd: 'I find getting killed preferable.'

In life, misery stands with its fangs bared right next to happiness. The same words that caused so much merriment now felt like the end to a tragic play. In Ramana's distorted writing they looked like 'I find Sakina's kisses preferable'.

Those who heard Gurudasa were jolted into alertness. The happy clamour of the group made way for low murmurs. Since Gurudasa had read the earlier part of the letter comfortably, what he read now had the ring of authority. To be clear, he read the whole sentence from the beginning: 'I find getting killed preferable to falling into the hands of the police.'

It was like a bucket of cold water had been flung on everyone. The mood turned sombre. No one knew exactly what Ramana was writing about, but it was clear that it was bad news. The men murmured among themselves.

As if he was determined to perform his duty, Gurudasa read two more sentences in a detached tone: 'I don't know if you will ever see me again. My property must be disposed of as below.'

Appa shot to his feet when he heard this and looked towards Antanna.

Antanna jumped up shouting, 'Ei, what are you reading? This is rubbish. Inauspicious. Enough of this now. Give it to me. You've taken the joke too far.'

Gurudasa mumbled the next line even as Antanna snatched the letter from him. 'I am living with someone here.'

The situation had turned so quickly that the men did not know how to respond. They stood around blankly. Antanna rushed into the house with the letter. Appa followed him.

After the ferocity of Antanna's reaction, no one needed to be told it was not a good idea to stay longer. Word reached the women as a broad summary: 'There's some bad news in Ramana's letter apparently.' Guradasa, who had read the letter and knew the horror of its contents, jumped on his bicycle and disappeared.

The cooks and helpers had been working since morning and were only then finishing their lunch. Antanna and Appa secreted the letter inside and emerged glowering. Word had reached Amma by then and she rushed there limping, asking, 'What? What happened?' Appa said something to keep her quiet for the time being. The house went from exuberance to gloom in the matter of a few minutes. Guests left hurriedly. Venu-mami did not wait for tea. The house was soon empty.

Appa and Antanna sat on a mat in the hall with Ramana's letter. Amma and I sat on another mat resting against the opposite wall. No one had answers to Amma's frightened questions. 'I can only tell you when I know,' Appa snapped. Appa and Antanna tried frantically to read the letter and after a while passed it to us, saying, 'See what you make of it.' I could not discern a single alphabet. Some way down the page, 'Sakina's kiss' stood out like a grinning apparition amidst Ramana's squiggles. I handed the letter back. Amma sat wiping her tears, not even wanting to look at the letter.

'Should we call Gurudasa?' Antanna asked.

Appa said, 'It's better not to hear about a family matter from an outsider.'

'I should never have brought the letter outside,' Antanna said.

We passed the letter back and forth for the next few hours, trying to make sense of it. With the mood around the letter having changed, what we saw in it was different too. Words related to death and dying suggested themselves with alarming frequency.

Amma heated up leftovers from the afternoon. We picked at the food. She had been hard at work since early in the morning but showed no signs of being tired or sleepy.

By nine we had worked out the crucial parts of the letter. Its contents were not well organized. Ramana seemed to have put down his thoughts in a hurry.

I have gone underground on some very important work. The police are looking for me. They will definitely come home to make inquiries. I will not allow myself to be captured. I find getting killed preferable to falling into the hands of the police. I am not scared of getting killed while fighting for what is right.

I don't know if you will ever see me again. My property must be disposed of as below. I am living with someone here. We are not married. Give everything to her if she ever comes looking for you. I am not writing her name here on purpose. There should be no injustice done to her. If she does not come, then distribute it among our four workers. Take care of your leg. If you have any of my previous letters, burn them at once. Most importantly, don't let the addresses at which you have written to me fall into anyone's hands. If you have them written down somewhere, burn them too. They should find nothing connected to me in the house. I have lived under different names, and it feels like that has changed who I am too. I'm proud that this short life could be dedicated to a worthy cause. Only you will appreciate the importance of this.

It was ominous that this letter did not end with the Golden Words that Appa always joked about. 'We should have read the letter as soon as it arrived,' Antanna said. The silence from the rest of us signalled our agreement. Amma went sobbing to the puja room.

Thankfully she didn't hear Appa muttering, 'Boon to others, bane to his own. His property it seems.'

At dawn Antanna removed all the letters from the wire. It was not hard to separate Ramana's letters from the rest. Appa and Antanna sat in front of the boiler in the bathroom. Amma and I stood behind them. Appa quickly looked over each one of the letters before consigning them to the flames. They burnt the letters as if they were permanently erasing Ramana's existence from our house. It reminded me of a funeral pyre.

What happened over the next few days was more terrible. Two plainclothes policemen came home the day after we burned the letters. They questioned us the same way pockets are turned inside out while looking for something. The family members and workers told the police that Ramana spent most of his time with me when he visited during his vacations. So the police went round and round and took me aside for questioning quite a few times. I learnt there was no end to how minutely a person's daily activities could be scrutinized.

What do you mean by 'reading'? Books or papers of some sort?

If he was reading a different book every day, there should be a lot of books in your house. Where are they? Why can't we see them?

He took them all without leaving a single book behind?

What other book titles can you recall?

So he never went to the plantation to work?

What did he do during the day?

Haha, nice. So he would make fun of himself by saying his was an eat-sleep-shit kind of life?

What time did he go to bed?

Ten every night?

Hmm, so different times. Did he do anything specific on the nights he went to bed late?

When they latched on to something, their questions and counter-questions elicited details I didn't even know I remembered.

No, Ramana did not sleep at ten every night. If he was reading, there was no telling how long he might stay up. He rose before anyone else at home. The first floor had two rooms on either side of the hall. The room on the right was Ramana's. It held none of his possessions when he was not occupying it. He brought a small bag with him when he visited. It held two shirts, two trousers, two dhotis, a thin towel and a couple of handkerchiefs. Half-sleeved shirts and cotton trousers that fit loosely, like pyjamas. I liked his style – wrinkled, unironed trousers. What space remained was all taken up by books. His mattress was placed next to the wall. He would read sitting with his back against the wall, legs folded under him. I once saw the name Orwell on one of his books. I don't remember anything else about them. The books were old, as if they had been read many times. Most were covered with newspaper. Other than what he was reading, his books stayed in his bag. He parted his hair on the left side. Curly. No, he did not apply oil to his hair. He had thick eyebrows that met in the middle. A thin, straight nose. He sometimes discussed cooking with Amma. He was a good cook. He did not regularly take tea or coffee.

When did I last speak to him, they wanted to know. As much as I tried, I could not recall the last thing he had said to me. Maybe it was while walking in the plantation on the day he had left, when he had said, 'Weeds and fallen leaves should

not be removed. They turn into good manure after a while.' Or
was it when he leaned and peered into the well: 'The water level
has dropped.' Which was earlier?

Amma cried whenever she was questioned. She could not
contain her grief when she recalled Ramana's favourite foods
and how he insisted on washing his own clothes. She brought
up incidents unrelated to the questions to give examples of his
goodness. Appa cautioned her: 'Stop crying and answer just as
much as you are asked.' But the police didn't seem to mind.
Amma even made tea for them. Then they had lunch at our
house, ate not one but two bananas each and resumed their
questioning.

It was only Amma who had any real affection for Ramana.
She alone took his side while talking to the police. He may
have been family, but the rest of us abandoned him the second
the police applied the slightest pressure. And we did so wearing
the cloak of virtue. Of course, the law had to be followed. Of
course, violence was unacceptable.

When Amma confronted the police, it was Antanna
who said in a low voice, 'Don't you know you're talking
to the police?' The note of surrender in his voice was new
and alarming.

'Can they be unjust simply because they are the police?'

'He has gone against the government. He will take us down
with him.' Antanna glared at her.

Appa tried to be conciliatory: 'Don't get into this. Leave it
to us.'

'First tell me where he is,' Amma said to the policemen.

'We are looking for him. That's why we need your help.
Tell us everything. Did he have any habits? Anything he did

every day without fail? Anything he could not do without? A specific hair oil? Cigarettes? What soap did he use?'

Could a man on the run in this vast world really be apprehended using such tiny details? Who knew, maybe one inconsequential fact could combine with another and turn into a definite lead.

'Who were his friends? Did he mention any names?'

I said, 'Orwell. Shakespeare. Marx.'

'Give us names from our country, son,' one of them said. 'Tell us about his girlfriends. He has one apparently,' he said and laughed.

'Allu Sarita.'

They were stunned. They made me say it again. I had no idea how I knew the name.

One of them said to the other in English, 'This boy is a gold mine.'

They continued to dig. I must have cooperated more than was required of me. They cajoled and flattered me so much that it was never clear if I was telling them the truth or whatever they wanted to hear. Going by their reaction when I said the name Sarita, they had been on her trail for quite some time.

'Try to remember,' they urged. 'How did her name come up?'

When I couldn't tell them anything more, they supplied details and looked to me for confirmation. I remember nodding when they asked, 'They were together in Hanamkonda, weren't they?'

'Was it just the two of them, or was there another person with them?'

In a flash I remembered when Ramana had said her name. Every year the people of our village came together to perform a play. That year's production had a particularly catchy song with the Kannada word 'allu' in the chorus. Ramana heard me singing it to myself and said, 'I know someone named Allu Sarita. She makes a pickle that sets your body on fire if even a little bit touches the tip of your tongue.'

'Sets your body on fire it seems. He's not talking about pickle, the horny bastard,' one of them said.

They teased out details, making me repeat them endlessly until a clear picture formed in my mind about events that I had been unable to remember earlier. By the time they were finished, I was convinced those events could not possibly have happened any other way. If the police did manage to catch Ramana, I don't know exactly what it was I said that led them to him. But I must have given them enough information. We received no letters from Ramana after that. Nor did we ever see him again. Strangely, the police did not ask me a single question about his letters. Maybe those questions were directed towards others in the family. I never found out what Appa and Antanna told them.

Despite all that I had said, I did not tell the police everything. Specifically, some of my conversations with Ramana. Like the police, Ramana too was adept at asking hundreds of specific questions and weaving the answers into something larger. When I told him about my ambition to study engineering and find a job in the city, he said, gravely, 'You are aspiring to a dull and ordinary life. What is there to it? Anyone can go with the flow and count their salary as they drift along. I could have done that too. Shamelessly grabbing the opportunities extended by an unjust system is the worst form of corruption. And then we justify such behaviour with words like "fairness" and "merit". Do something that changes the course of people's lives. There's meaning in that.'

The word 'dull' pierced me to my core. It was insulting to be told my life's ambition was commonplace and uninspired. Even corrupt apparently. It made no sense to me to give up existing comforts and actively seek out hardship. I thought of the people who flocked to Ramana every time he came to the village and asked him to accompany them to government offices. I said, 'I have no interest in politics.'

Ramana laughed. I thought it was a contemptuous laugh. 'If you want to escape politics, you might as well stay at home and take to bed,' he said. 'It's everywhere, even if you don't see it.'

'What can I do by myself?'

'A house is built with thousands of bricks. But removing ten bricks creates a hole wide enough to let someone in. Never forget this. Ten people coming together is enough.' He held up his open palms and wiggled his fingers.

Before they left, the police described the activities of Ramana and his group in brutal detail. This caused Amma a great deal of distress. 'Impossible,' she protested. 'You must be mistaken. He's the kind of boy who can't kill an ant.'

'You keep quiet,' Appa said sternly. 'Women shouldn't interfere.'

The police justified their brutality saying it was a matter of survival. 'We are not making any of this up. These are well-educated people who become involved in violent activities. Should we stand by with our hands folded when it is a

question of our lives?' The stories they told were so savage
they defied belief.

One night, a group forcibly entered a policeman's house,
tied up his wife and children and shot him. He was badly
injured, and though he asked them to kill him, they left him
half-alive. He died slowly, begging all night for water while his
family looked on helplessly.

'That attack was led by your compassionate Ramana. We
will get him. And we will teach a lesson to those who helped
him go undercover. The bastard thinks he can get away after
killing a policeman. We're watching all of you. It's over when
we find him. He's not big enough to be protected. When a
fleck of dirt gets into our eye, we don't rest until it is removed.'

After they left, their visit haunted Amma day and night.
I saw how invisible sorrow can eat up a person from within like
termites. I have no doubt this is the reason she lost her will to
live. From time to time, I reassured her, saying he would surely
return, but she must have known deep inside that her brother
was gone forever. I have never again in my life seen such an
intensity of grief, that is, such an intensity of love.

7

Rekha came at four in the afternoon.

Antanna let out a cry from the front yard. The joy and relief in his voice made it clear Rekha had returned. Viji was lying down beside me, looking at the roof. I said, 'Come, get up. The princess has come.'

Viji caught the annoyance in my voice and said, 'Don't shout at her in front of everyone. The important thing is that she's back. We can think of everything else later.'

Antanna was animatedly addressing one of the workers in the yard: 'Bring him here at once. Tell him we need four tender coconuts brought down urgently. Run!' Then he noticed us and tried to pretend he had said nothing.

Rekha, in jeans and a loose T-shirt, slipped off her backpack from her shoulders and left it by the door. Her expression did not change when she saw us. She said, 'So you came after me. Now I'm here. Lost and found.'

There wasn't the slightest trace of guilt for all that she had put us through. Instead, her tone suggested it was our fault that we had come all the way. Her hair was dishevelled, her face tanned from being out in the sun. Her T-shirt collar was damp with sweat. She sat down on the verandah to take off her shoes.

I waited for Viji to say something. I suspected Rekha had already met Suresh before coming home and this made me a little jealous.

'Come in now. Have you had lunch?' Viji asked.

'Yes, I've eaten. I just want to bathe and sleep. I am very tired.'

She picked up the bag and went inside without looking any of us in the eye. Viji went in after her. They both entered the bedroom, leaving the door ajar. I began to weigh the possibilities of returning by the night bus. I thought I should check with Viji before booking the ticket, pushed open the door and entered the room.

It was dark inside. Viji was sitting on a stool. Rekha was at the other end of the room with her back towards the door. She was rummaging inside her backpack, which she had laid on the bed. She took the clothes she wanted for her bath, hitched a combination lock to the zipper pulls and quickly turned its discs. That single, small act expressed her disaffection with us.

'There is a limit to everything,' Viji said, taking an ember to a chain of firecrackers.

'You're still a little girl. Keep that in mind,' I said, fully knowing that both those words, 'little' and 'girl', would annoy her. She said nothing.

We both pounced on her. It wasn't clear which of us said what.

'Do you think we won't interfere if you run around risking your life?'

'We have been suffering since yesterday. How could you go without telling us?'

'And we have boys from your college coming home to torment us. What are we supposed to think if you vanish at the same time?'

'First tell us where you went.'

'What kind of emergency? Was it so bad you had to go without telling your parents? As if only you people can save the world . . .'

'I had to fall at people's feet in office to take leave and rush here.'

'It's all his fault. He even lied shamelessly this morning and said he knew nothing.'

'Don't defend him! Don't we have eyes? One look at his face was enough to tell he was lying. Takes just one person to ruin an entire town.'

'Such people should be thrashed mercilessly. They like to shove other people's children into wells to check the depth.'

I said, 'We never treated you differently because you were a girl. That was our mistake.'

At any other time Rekha would have been outraged by my comment. There was no chance of that now. Her exhaustion was plain from her drawn face. I grew even more furious with Suresh.

Viji relented somewhat. 'Go take your bath. Sleep for some time.'

'Let's leave tonight,' I said. 'I'll book the tickets.'

I went to the hall, where a relieved Antanna was pottering about. 'Ask them to keep three tickets for the night bus,' I said.

Antanna left briskly, saying, 'We'll get the seats. It's only difficult on Saturdays.'

I threw down a mat in the front room and lay down. Soon I was asleep. I don't know what mother and daughter did after Rekha finished her bath. When I awoke, the door to the room was still ajar. I got up. As I approached the door, I could hear whispered conversation from within.

'Why be afraid? Let everything come out,' Rekha was saying.

'They should get what belongs to them. It's a question of doing the right thing.' I could barely discern Viji's words.

Rekha said something I could not hear. I pushed open the door. Rekha was lying on her back. Viji was on her side facing her. They looked like they had been talking for a long time.

'What are you talking about?' I asked.

'We must leave today. I was saying I can't afford to miss office tomorrow.'

They were clearly hiding something. I moved the door back to its almost-closed position, went over to the bed and sat on its edge. I thought Rekha must have told her everything when I was sleeping outside. I asked, 'What was this earth-shaking work you had to do without telling us?'

'I am not going to tell you. Stop asking.'

'How long will you keep it from us? We'll find out anyway after it is printed in that rag of his.'

'You don't have to wait until then. I will tell you myself when the time is right.'

Viji said, 'It's okay, leave it now. She'll tell us when she tells us.' Viji was taking her side. I was certain there was no connection between office tomorrow and the whispered words.

'Why be afraid?' she had said. Afraid of whom? Then the comment about doing the right thing.

I smarted from the insult of being kept out of their conversation. And I was furious. I said, 'What, mother and daughter are having a laugh? I don't want any of this. Stay away from him. Is that clear?' My voice grew louder as I spoke until I was almost shouting.

They were taken aback. Viji said after a moment, 'Don't imagine things. She's back and that's all that matters.'

Viji had joined me in rebuking Rekha not even an hour ago. Her manner had changed since then. I knew they had discussed something and kept me out. I said, 'It was wrong of her to go in the first place. And now she behaves like she has done us a big favour by returning. What is Suresh's role in all this? That slimy bastard. And those uncles who came to our house. Is he connected to them in some way? He must be. Loafers all of them. These media types are all blackmailers.'

'I can't believe I am hearing you say such things, Appa.'

'Then what, should I sing praises of the man who has used my daughter? Provoke me, and I can say worse.'

'There's no relation between the two.'

'Then tell us clearly what is going on.'

'Nothing.'

'Where had you gone?'

'I can't tell you.'

'As if he runs some great magazine. You don't understand these things.'

Viji interrupted: 'Leave it now. Don't go over the same thing again and again.'

'That means you know. Only I have been kept in the dark.'

'Unlike you I'm not desperate to know. If I start talking
about everything I know, life would become impossible.'

If I continued to argue I was bound to lose control. I got
up. Before leaving the room, I said, 'Let's eat something quickly
and go. We have a bus to catch.'

Rekha said, 'You both can go. I'll come after two days.'

'No,' I said sternly. 'The three of us are leaving together.
Today.'

Antanna appeared at the door. Rekha looked at him
pleadingly, but he did not go to her aid. 'It's better you go
today,' he said. 'Come back later. You saved my face by
returning today. I have now entrusted you to your father. It is
up to him.'

Rekha's face fell. I looked at her triumphantly as if to say
it served her right. Though I wavered for a moment on seeing
her downcast, there was no way I was going to leave her behind
in the village.

8

We left by the night bus at ten.

Viji and Rekha sat together, with Rekha by the window. I took the seat behind them. After we got on the bus Rekha put on her earphones, shut her eyes and rested her head against the windowpane, making conversation impossible.

The bus was dark except for the feeble blue light of the night-lamp at the front. I could not sleep. Rekha's antics had set a hundred questions racing in my mind. Where could she have gone? For what? Had she put herself in danger to impress Suresh? I recalled a newspaper article I had read a long time ago. It was about a young woman who had travelled deep into a forest to meet so-called revolutionaries and returned after spending a few days with them.

My mind began to invent scenarios for how Rekha had spent the last two days.

It is not easy to establish contact with people who are hiding from the police. Rekha must have passed on a message through a chain of contacts, received a reply, followed their instructions and made it to their hideout. My imagination flowed unchecked. Rekha leaves on the Bengaluru bus but gets off at a town in between and spends the night there. She takes another bus the next morning to a small village near the edge of a forest. She has been instructed to cover her head with a red dupatta while leaving the bus. Nothing happens for a while. Then an autorickshaw stops near her and the driver says, 'Madam, come with me. I will take you to Kailasa.' She recognizes the signal and gets in. He drops her off in front of a house on the outskirts of the village.

As she is crossing the gate, the front door opens. A woman. 'Where are you going?'

'Kailasa.'

The woman invites her in. It is the secret word that opens all doors. Rekha is blindfolded and taken to the hideout. She is tested in various ways to make sure she is not there under false pretences. Men surround her, asking if she is willing to sacrifice anything and everything for the struggle. She says yes. 'Even your virginity?' asks a voice. A man begins to finger her clothes.

My heart shuddered. My imagination could go no further. No, it couldn't possibly be like this. Everything I thought I knew came from dubious sources. A film I had watched, an article someone had written in a newspaper, things people had said on websites. I had given no thought to whether these sources were reliable. There was no need to. Who cares how we learn about situations we will never encounter? But now that I found myself in exactly such a situation, every detail was crucial. I was desperate to reach a definite conclusion. I had never imagined that Rekha could do anything like what she had just done. But then, neither had I seen Ramana, whom I had known so well, as capable of violence. None of us had bothered to question if what was said about him was really true. Such is the power of the state. It hands us threads and has us twist them into a rope that can later be used to hang us.

I made an effort to banish these useless thoughts from my mind. Sleep continued to prove elusive. I was worried for Rekha's future. I could picture her among girls who roamed about late at night with boys on motorcycles and in cars, who staggered out of pubs with an arm around some young man's waist. I could see her living by herself so she could do as she pleased, changing boyfriends on a whim, torturing us by not giving us her address. It's fine to talk about all sorts of freedoms when they are not at your throat. Now, with her own well-being in mind, it appeared best to set her on a path that would lead to her settling down in life. I found the idea of handing over her responsibility to a husband strangely comforting. I recall that during our wedding, several people came up to Viji's father and congratulated him after the *kanyadaana* rite during which she was entrusted to me. 'It's a burden off your mind,' they had said to him. Then I had thought this was nothing more than a platitude.

The bus shook the nights of the settlements it passed through. Some of the houses had dim lights left on in front of them.

I leaned forward in my seat and saw that Viji had slipped into sleep. The shawl she had pulled over herself partly covered

Rekha. It wasn't very cold, but, of course, the shawl was not really for the cold. The intimacy of sharing a blanket or shawl is something else entirely.

I dozed in brief spells. The shaking and rattling of the bus brought a vague awareness that distance was being covered. We reached Bengaluru at half past six in the morning. We didn't have the patience to negotiate with an autorickshaw driver, so we agreed to whatever was demanded and got in. Rekha sat between us, leaning forward so we were not packed too close. It was a little chilly now. Viji extended the shawl she was wearing over Rekha and tried to protect her from the cold air rushing in from both sides. That forest she went to, was it cold there too? Or maybe it was raining. Had she even gone to a forest? My thoughts were stuck in this groove.

After we had travelled some distance, I noticed that Rekha had nodded off. I felt a surge of affection. I should sit with her and explain that for all my sternness I was really on her side. I was a bitter pill she had to swallow for her own good. Knowing her, she would probably make fun of me for saying such a thing.

We reached home at seven. As we got out of the lift at our floor, I opened the side pocket of my bag and began rummaging for the house key. It evaded my hand for a brief while. Viji and Rekha stood impatiently at the door till I found it.

'Couldn't you have got it out earlier and kept it ready?' Viji said.

I slipped the key into the keyhole and turned it through two clicks to release the lock. Then, as usual, I pushed the door gently. It did not open.

'Open it quickly!' Viji said. 'I need to use the toilet. This is the trouble with bus journeys. You men won't understand – you just stand and let loose wherever you want.'

I pushed the door. Then I pushed it harder. It didn't yield. I inserted the key again, locked the door noisily, and, as if trying to reassure the lock that everything was fine, turned my wrist as smoothly as I could. This time I applied my weight on the door and pushed. It didn't budge.

'Move, I'll open it,' Viji said.

I gave her the key and stepped aside. The thought struck me just as she was about to turn the key: 'I think the door is bolted from inside.'

Viji looked alarmed. 'How can that be? This is the only way in.'

'Then why isn't it opening?'

I examined the outside of the door. I locked and unlocked it again. It still would not open. I banged on the door. 'Who's there?' I called. I wanted to shout louder but didn't want to wake any neighbours who might be sleeping. I didn't even know if there really was someone inside or if the lock was just acting up.

We stood outside our own house knocking on the door. Viji rang the bell a few times. No one answered.

'This is not a problem with the lock,' I said. 'The bolt inside has fallen into place.'

'What do you mean "fallen"?' Viji asked. 'That bolt needs to be pushed up. We use it only while locking up for the night. Do you think there's someone inside?'

'Let's all three of us try to push the door,' I said. Rekha moved into position next to the two of us and put her palms

on the door. 'When I say . . . gaja . . . bhuja . . . bala . . .' We
pushed with all our strength. It had been many years since I
had invoked my mantra, but it did not help.

I had been longing for the familiarity of home after the
chaos and stress of the last few days. Now this absurd situation
had stopped me at my own doorstep. I was disgusted.

'Wait, I'll bring the watchman,' Rekha said and ran down
the stairs. She reappeared in the lift accompanied by the
watchman.

He shuffled over from the lift with absolutely no urgency
or interest. I felt my temper rising at his lethargy. 'It's bolted
from inside,' I said. 'The door isn't opening.'

'How can that be, saab?' he asked. 'All three of you are
outside. Who can bolt it?'

'That's why we called you. Maybe there's someone inside.'

My voice had risen without my knowledge. The door
of the flat next to ours opened and Fernandes emerged to
check what the commotion so early in the morning was
about. I told him what had happened. Next, the door on
the opposite side opened. Kashyap and his wife peeped out.
Fernandes enthusiastically repeated everything I had just
told him.

'We have an old pestle used for pounding grain. It's perfect
for forcing open the door,' Kashyap's wife offered helpfully.
Viji asked to use their toilet and rushed into their flat.

Next, Ranjoy, from the last remaining flat on our floor,
appeared on the scene. All the men tried the door one after the
other and independently concluded it was bolted from within.
Aniruddh from the floor below came up the steps and joined
the group's deliberations.

'There are so many of us. If he runs out now, he is sure to be caught.'

'What if he has a knife?'

'How many people can he stab? One at most.'

'All right. You stand in the front.'

They all laughed.

I was annoyed the situation had turned into a source of entertainment. There seemed no way out but to break open the door. Kashyap went to his flat and returned brandishing a stout wooden pestle tipped with iron. It was almost as tall as he was. By then half the occupants of the building were crowded in the passage. The watchman stood to one side, looking dazed, talking to no one in particular: 'There is only one door. He has bolted it and now he is trapped inside.'

Aniruddh, youngest among us and the strongest built, took the pestle and hefted it with enthusiasm. A bunch of discoloured threads was tied around his right wrist. Kashyap's wife gushed about the pestle: 'We brought it from my mother-in-law's house. It must be more than seventy years old.' Then, there was the question of how exactly the door was to be broken. Everyone began to issue instructions. Aniruddh raised the pestle and sized up the door as he decided where to strike first.

'Wait, wait,' Ranjoy cried from somewhere at the back. 'I know how to do this. Don't break the door, I'm coming,' he said and sidled his way up through the crowd. He placed a hand on Aniruddh's arm and stopped him. 'Hit the door repeatedly near the bolt,' he said. 'Do it through a thick layer of cloth, and strike exactly over the bolt. Otherwise the door will splinter.'

In the light of such clear and confident instructions, an old towel was brought from Kashyap's flat and wrapped around one end of the pestle. I visualized how I dangled the milk bag outside, locked the door and slid the bolt, and put my hand on the door where I guessed the bolt to be.

'Make sure the door is unlocked,' Ranjoy said. I confirmed that it was.

Aniruddh invoked the patron deity of wrestlers and body-builders and cried 'Jai Hanuman' through clenched teeth as he rammed the pestle into the door where I had indicated. More than the force of the blow, it felt like his battle cry had worked. The bolt snapped and the door swung open gently. There wasn't a scratch on it. We now knew for a fact that the door had been bolted from within. A few voices sounded disappointed that the operation had ended so quickly: 'What? It's open? Just one blow?' Ranjoy, who had provided the know-how, looked around beaming.

The light in the hall was faint. Everything appeared still. I opened the door fully. Despite the bravado that had been on display, those at the front took a step back. Standing at the doorstep I reached in and turned on the lights. There was no one there.

'Don't go in,' Viji said to me.

Everyone stood peering into the hall as if something dramatic was about to occur. Aniruddh stood by the door with the pestle raised above his head in case someone ran out. After some time had passed, someone from behind said, 'Watchman, go in and look around once.'

The watchman was reluctant. He may have been the building's security guard, but he was not about to wander into a dangerous situation carrying only a stick. 'What if there is someone there?' he asked.

'That is why we are asking you to go in,' a voice in the crowd said, setting off a ripple of laughter.

When a couple of minutes went by without any noise from within, I cautiously took a step into the hall.

'Careful,' someone said from behind. 'Thieves never come alone.'

The first thing I did was make sure there was no one hiding behind the door. This seemed to embolden the watchman. He pounded his stick on the ground a few times and came forward. 'Let me take a look, sir,' he said. He curtly asked Viji to step aside, as if he had been held back until then only because she was in the way.

'Is there anyone inside? Please come out,' I said loudly.

My request was hardly going to strike terror in the heart of a thief hiding inside. The watchman took a few steps into the hall, pounding his stick at intervals, and shouted almost as a formality: 'Listen, you swine. Come out now. I am going to smash your face.' It was obvious his anger was feigned. There was no sound or movement from within the house. The onlookers waited at the door with some mixture of excitement and apprehension. Newcomers were brought up to speed by those who had arrived earlier.

The watchman grew braver on not receiving a response. He went to the kitchen and peeped inside. He stood at the doorways of the bedrooms and looked around. 'There's no one here, sir,' he called out.

I realized he hadn't checked the bathrooms. But if I told him, he would enter the bathrooms wearing shoes, so I decided to go myself.

I went quickly from room to room, looking over each one to see if anything was out of place. As soon as I stepped into the bathroom attached to our bedroom, I saw that the windowpane had been cut out. A rope, knotted at intervals, was visible at the window.

'Look here!' I shouted. 'This is where they entered.' Viji, Rekha and the watchman rushed over.

'Very smart people,' the watchman said. 'If they climb down this side of the building, it's not possible to see them even during the day.' Clearly he was praising the thieves to prevent blame from coming his way.

Voices saying 'From where? How?' indicated the crowd outside had now begun to stream into the house. They looked around curiously. Even ordinary objects acquire a different meaning when seen as part of someone else's life. A few were unable to resist taking a quick tour of the kitchen. Everyone wanted to see for themselves where the thieves had entered. Soon, there was a crowd in the bathroom. Looking at our bathroom through the eyes of others I found it shabby. The shower curtain had blotches from all the water it had seen. The wall tiles were grimy at the joints. Stuck to the soap-tray were the remains of many generations of soap. Viji must have felt a similar discomfort. She moved a tub of unwashed clothes to the bedroom and covered it with a towel.

I heard Kashyap calling out urgently to me from the kitchen. I rushed there to find that he and his wife were closely examining our vermicelli maker. 'Where did you buy this?' he asked delightedly. 'I've been looking for a good one for a long time now.'

This was hardly the time or place. I felt my blood boil. 'I don't know,' I snapped and went to the bedroom.

While entering the room this time, I noticed that the keys of the large steel almirah where we kept all our valuables were dangling from its lock. I shouted for Viji. Neither of us could say if we had left the keys there in our rush or if the thieves had unlocked the almirah. I reached out to open it and realized just in time that the handle might have fingerprints on it. I used my handkerchief to open the door. The inside of the almirah was as usual a mess. It was impossible to say at a glance if anything was missing.

Viji and I were startled by a high-pitched voice asking, 'How much is gone?' It was Vasantibai, the woman who lived alone on the ground floor. She was standing right behind us, grinning. Her greying hair was dishevelled, and it looked like she had come straight from bed. She was staring unblinkingly into the almirah. I slammed the door shut. Viji said, 'No, no, nothing,' but Vasantibai opened her eyes wide and raised her eyebrows like she didn't believe her. I had never seen her at such close range before. I was disgusted by her facial expressions and the strands of grey hair on her chin. I saw that Vasantibai was wearing her slippers and lost my temper. 'You should not be wearing footwear in here. Will you tolerate it if someone enters your house like that?'

She was not perturbed. She pointed a finger towards the hall and said, 'But so many people are wearing footwear. If I don't wear slippers my legs ache from the cold.'

'I will tell them too. First you get those slippers off.'

The crowd gathered in the house was by now creating a commotion. It looked more like a party than the scene of a break-in. Rekha had gone to her room, closed the door most of the way and was busy with something at her table. She could be seen through the gap in the door, her preoccupied manner discouraging anyone from entering.

The group in the hall was talking about the precautions they had taken against their flats being broken into. Kashyap was boasting about how he had had an iron grill fixed on all windows, be it bedroom or bathroom.

Ground-floor D'Souza's attention wandered towards the watchman. 'Should we not be asking what the watchmen were doing? If a thief can descend from the terrace, roam around inside one of our houses and then climb down and disappear without the watchmen noticing, why do we have them at all? If such people are allowed to protect the country, we will be finished.' In his youth D'Souza had worked as a supplier to a military canteen. This qualified him to hold forth whenever the subject of security came up, be it of the building or the nation.

Ramesh, who was a lawyer, joined in. 'Last week I went to watch the night show of a film. They were both fast asleep when I returned. It was impossible to wake them. When they finally opened the gate, they glared at me like it was my fault for disturbing their sleep. The bottom line is that we have to take care of our own houses.'

'Where is our building association president, Mr Sharma? The security people must be trembling now that he's going to shout at them.' Those who caught D'Souza's sarcasm could not control their laughter. Sharma was a hopelessly mild-mannered man.

'Sharma is not in town,' Aniruddh said. 'He will be back in two days. Colonel sahib is also away.' He was still walking around the hall with the pestle in his hand. Kashyap's wife hovered about him, unsure whether the pestle's work was done, looking for an opportune moment to take it back.

Mrs Kamat said to Aniruddh, 'I was shocked when you broke open the door with just one blow. It gave way so easily. The bolts in our houses must be really strong!'

Aniruddh was still glowing from the display of his prowess. He said, 'I didn't even need this actually. I could have just hit the door with my hand.'

'You must have a lot of practice,' Mrs Kamat said. It was only when everyone burst into laughter that Anriuddh realized that she was pulling his leg.

The watchman returned from his inspection of the terrace. 'They've climbed down from the terrace and gone back up. There's no rope going down.'

D'Souza burst out: 'Did they get to the terrace by falling from the sky? They entered through the gate and left through the gate while the two of you were grazing donkeys.'

The watchman squirmed. His face fell. There was no doubt that when the police came, they would start their investigation with the building's watchmen. It was standard practice for watchmen to be roughed up a little when there was a robbery. And if they went into hiding to avoid it, the police immediately concluded they were guilty.

I asked in a loud voice, piercing the scattered conversations in the room, 'Who has the police station's number? Does anyone know who the inspector is?'

Ramesh came forward smartly, knowing this was his area of expertise. 'Calling them on the phone is useless. If you catch hold of a thief they'll come running, but they won't bother if a robbery has already taken place. Best to go personally to the station. The inspector is a good man. He spoke nicely when I went to report that my son's mobile was missing. The mobile was never found, but even then . . . You know where the station is, just four crosses down the road.'

Giri Rao, who had been quiet until now, joined in: 'You have just returned. Have some tea and rest for a while. Then check if any cash or gold is missing. That's what the police will want to know. Give them the details. It will be useful if the thieves are caught one day. Do you have insurance?'

I said, in earnest, 'We don't keep cash or gold in the house. Nothing seems to be missing so far.'

As soon as I turned away, I overheard Giri Rao say to someone, 'See how he brushed away the question. Which house doesn't have a little cash or gold? People say such things to comfort themselves. Or maybe there was cash they can't tell the police about.' I pretended not to have heard him.

I felt like I would go mad if I didn't send them all away immediately. 'I am calling the police now,' I said. 'There will be confusion if they find fingerprints of people who don't live here. And the dogs might lead them to your houses if you stay here for a long time. So please clear the flat now and don't touch anything. Very, very grateful to everyone. We troubled you so early in the morning.'

Before leaving D'Souza said to me: 'This is definitely the work of someone known to you. Think about who knew you were away. I'm not accusing anyone, just asking you to think about it.'

People began to shuffle out. I went to close the front door behind them and then thought this might appear rude. So I swung it shut most of the way. We had the house to ourselves in a few minutes. At the upper corner of the door, sticking out like a tiny flag, was the socket that had been torn out of the door frame with the bolt inside. I eased the ring off the finger, slid the bolt down and shut the door.

Before leaving the village, both Viji and I had planned to go to office in the morning. But I was not sure after this new development. If our daily wheel was to turn as usual, it needed to have been set in motion by now. I went to Viji, who was pacing in the kitchen. She was clearly distressed by the break-in. She said, 'Who knows what they have touched here. I feel like throwing out everything. What could they have wanted?'

I too had a vague feeling that things were out of place. Now that we were looking closely at every object in the house, we could not be sure what we had left a certain way and what the intruders might have displaced. Did we always keep the tongs in that corner of the kitchen counter? Had the plastic holder in which we left washed spoons to dry moved a little to the right? Had we left these cups in the sink? Didn't we always make sure the sugar tin was inside the cabinet? What had this empty plastic box held? Because we knew someone else had been in our house, things we had barely noticed until then grew prominent. We saw the familiar with newly suspicious eyes.

D'Souza's parting comment came to mind. I said to Viji: 'Those people who came the other day, MP3's uncles. Do you think they are somehow connected with this?'

'I don't know what to think. God only knows.'

'I'm going to take leave. Don't know how long it will take in the police station. And I haven't slept properly these last two nights. You can't stay at home today?'

Viji said, 'No, I have an important meeting. Maybe I can go a little late.'

Rekha casually said she would be going to college. It rankled to see her behave as if what was going on at home was of no concern to her.

'Be careful,' I said. 'I'm worried about those people who visited the other day. They're dangerous.' I knew this would provoke her.

Rekha lost her temper. 'You're a coward, Appa,' she said. 'You're scared of people from that class, that's all. MP3 is dumb but he's not dangerous. Those uncles are hangers-on who run around on behalf of this useless fellow whenever he thinks he is in love. They had gone to Sarala's house too. Her father made a scene and called the police. They gave up after that. The same thing happened with Veena. Now he's after me. He's probably moved on to someone else by now. No messages in the last two days. Otherwise he was eating my head night and day, offering all kinds of expensive gifts. It made me laugh, that's all. I feel sorry for him, but there's nothing to be scared of.'

While speaking to me Rekha had, for a moment, turned to look at Viji. I didn't know what that fleeting glance between them meant. 'Let them go to anyone else's house,' I said. 'What worries me is that they came to ours.'

Rekha went to her room without saying more.

'Better to keep the house as it is until the police come. I'll go to the police station now,' I said.

'Pack some breakfast on your way back,' Viji said.

'Idli-vada will do?'

Viji nodded absent-mindedly.

I went to the door of Rekha's room and said, 'Idli and vada?' She was stuffing something into her backpack. I was going to ask what it was, but then saw her frown and kept quiet. No matter how grown up your children are, it is difficult to accept that they keep certain things from you.

'I don't want anything,' she said. 'Bring some bread and I'll make myself a sandwich.' And then, as if replying to what I would have said next, she added: 'All right, bring what you want. I'll eat it.'

* * *

'The idli is still so hot,' I said as I unwrapped the packets on the dining table.

Viji said, 'What happened at the police station?'

'The sub-inspector was not around. Someone else, a head constable I think, heard me out. The police station was not what I expected at all. They were very polite. When their tea came, they offered me a cup too.'

Rekha said, 'Don't forget, it's the same place where they thrash people to death.'

I ignored her and went on: 'I was a bit anxious, but they must see cases like this every day. The head constable listened to me patiently. When I mentioned the building's name, he asked, "Isn't Sharma the society president?" I don't know how he knew. It seems there have been three complaints from our area in just the last week. But this is the first time a flat has been broken into. He said apartment buildings are harder to target – even if there's no CCTV, there are people around. He asked some questions – had the watchman quit, where we had gone, for what purpose. Like a fool I asked if they were going to bring dogs. "How much is gone? Cash or gold?" he asked. When I told him he said they only use the dog squad for major burglaries. Anyway, they will send someone. We need to write out a complaint.'

'Okay, what then?' Viji asked. Her tone indicated she expected me to handle the situation.

'Let them come and take a look first. We'll see what they say.'

The three of us had barely finished breakfast and gone to our rooms when the bell rang. Two policemen were at the door. One of them said, 'Namaskara, sir. I am Rudrayya. The inspector has sent me.'

I invited them in. Rudrayya did all the talking. The other stayed silent and looked around. I asked him what his name was. He said, 'Channappa, sir.' It was clear that Rudrayya was the senior among the two. He led the way; Channappa followed. Rudrayya spoke; Channappa agreed.

I told them the whole story: how we went to the village, how we returned in the morning to find the door bolted from inside, how we broke open the door and what we found inside. The house, showing no obvious signs of being burgled, did not appear to make an impression on them. Rudrayya looked around the hall carefully and began to ask questions.

'How did they enter?'

'Through the bathroom window.'

'Show us.'

We entered our bedroom, where Viji was sitting on the bed looking at her phone. 'Namaskara, madam,' Rudrayya said. Viji stood up and joined her palms in a namaste.

Rudrayya examined the bathroom. He went 'Mmm . . . Mmm' when he saw the skill with which the thieves had broken in, carefully cutting out the windowpane and placing it to one side. It was not clear if this was just a mannerism or if he was actually appreciating the thieves.

'What has been taken?' Rudrayya asked disinterestedly.

'We haven't found anything missing so far. Everything seems as it was. No idea why they came.'

A knowing smile flickered on Rudrayya's face. He said, 'Amateurs try to open almirahs and locked trunks. Experienced thieves don't waste their time. They grab money from the most unlikely places in the house as if they had hidden it there themselves. They don't touch anything else. The minds of these thieves and their victims work the same way.'

I wondered what he was implying.

'Have you made an estimate of what is missing, madam?' he asked Viji. He had already asked me the question and was now asking it to Viji in front of me.

She said, 'We don't keep gold in the house. There was no cash. We need to check if anything else is missing.'

'Does the building have CCTV?'

'No, we haven't installed it yet.'

'Where do you work, sir?'

I told him the name of my company.

'I only asked because people with dirty money always say in their complaint that nothing is missing, but they come running with a long list when the thief is caught. These are well-connected people, so we start getting phone calls from above. Becomes a big problem for us.'

Channappa began to speak: 'In one case they took only Hindustani music CDs. Another fellow left behind all other drinks and only took bottles of whisky.' Talk turned to the strange ways of thieves. The presence of a woman seemed to have made them more forthcoming.

Rudrayya reined in Channappa's enthusiasm by sending him away – 'Go to the terrace and see how they lowered the rope' – and started on another story.

'They all get caught one day or the other. I've seen all kinds during my service. One day, I went to help this fellow who was changing a scooter tyre by the side of the road. He saw me and ran. I caught him after a chase. Then he began to tell me about his exploits.'

Channappa returned. He said, 'They climbed down neatly from the terrace.'

Viji said appreciatively, 'Even the bathroom glass has been removed carefully, without breaking it.'

This led to a technical explanation from Rudrayya. 'They first apply adhesive tape to the glass and make a kind of handle. Then they run a glass cutter around it. The cut portion comes away silently when they tug it using the handle. If only they used this intelligence for something good . . .'

'Thank god we were not at home,' Viji said.

'Aiyo madam, they will walk through a house when its residents are sleeping. Sometimes they try to get an almirah key from under a pillow. People have woken up and thieves have been caught like this.'

Rudrayya saw the alarm and disgust on Viji's face when she imagined strangers walking around the house while she slept. He laughed self-importantly. 'Do you suspect anyone?' he asked. 'Have you had any repair work done recently? Plumbing? Any fights? Any business deals gone wrong?'

'No, nothing like that. We don't suspect anyone,' I said. MP3 and his uncles came to mind, but I decided it was not the time to bring them up.

'I am asking because no one breaks into a house without good reason. They come looking for something. It doesn't have to be money. Give it some thought. See if anything comes to mind.'

I remained silent.

'All right, sir. Make a list of everything that is missing and write out a complaint by evening. We'll take care of the rest. Take my number. If it ends up becoming a big case, we can look at CCTV from neighbouring streets. That takes time. If you don't hide anything, we may be able to help you.' I saved Rudrayya's number on my phone, and they both left after shaking my hand.

Viji and Rekha came to the hall.

'What should we do now?' I said loudly to myself, but also addressing Rekha and Viji.

'Why should we file a complaint?' Viji asked. 'We imagine there will be police dogs and special forces running around with guns, but what you get are two bored constables.'

'Someone breaking and entering our house is a good enough reason to file a complaint. Rekha, check your room and see if anything is missing.'

'What is in my room? All junk. Left to me I would keep a few clothes and throw everything else out. It saves me the trouble if they've taken anything.'

'Let us take this as an opportunity and clean up the house. We can give away whatever we don't use.'

'Please, Appa. Stop it. This is your positive attitude nonsense. Who will take this junk from us even if we offer it for free?'

My silence further enraged her. 'See whatever you want to see as an opportunity, but leave me alone. I haven't slept as it is, and now I have to go to college.'

I decided not to provoke her. 'I've taken leave today,' I said. 'I'll go through the house carefully. I can't bear to think a stranger has wandered aimlessly through the house. I will feel better if it turns out something is missing.'

'All of us can't leave work and sit at home. If I see Jaishankar in office, I'll ask him to put in a word with the commissioner. Maybe they'll do a better job of investigating. In any case, it's better not to let the police loose without any direction. You never know where they'll take the matter. I'm going for a bath now,' Viji said and hurried off.

I noticed that Rekha went to her room lost in her phone and pushed the door shut with one foot.

9

With Viji and Rekha gone for the day, it is time to begin my inventory of the house. I can't decide where to start, so I make myself a cup of tea and sit in the hall. The first place my attention goes to is the cabinet filled with books. The broker who showed me the flat had called it a showcase. Every house in the building has one of these. Invariably, they are used to display objects that reflect the success and well-being of the family. Photographs of children and grandchildren attest to an untroubled family life. Strange dolls and figurines are evidence of international travel or at least connections to foreign lands. Some have cups and trophies from sporting victories, others have framed certificates. There are even those who think a sparkling tea set in the showcase signifies a life of comfort and indulgence.

One day, Kashyap, who cannot find a book in his house to save his life, came home to hand over some papers. He looked at our showcase and chided us: 'What is this? Full of books.

You have spoiled the show of the showcase.' Viji and I made
fun of his taste for a long time after that. We told the story at
parties and among friends and got laughs out of it. But sitting
here in the hall with my cup of tea, it strikes me that in making
fun of Kashyap, we did not behave any differently from my
colleagues who mocked my taste in reading.

I get up and stand in front of the showcase. I am astonished
by just how many books I have acquired over the years. Some
are even stuffed horizontally above other books. It has been
ages since I looked at them. There are books here that are over
twenty years old. What purpose can there be in keeping them?
At one point, I tried to eliminate the word 'purpose' from my
vocabulary after reading a book. *Beware of Purpose* must be here
somewhere. *Fight Smarter* too.

Now the books feel like a desperate attempt to cover up
defects within me, to compensate for something inside that
was broken. Whatever those defects, they don't seem quite as
bad any more. We live in a time when people shamelessly put
their prejudices, narcissism and depravity on display, when it is
possible to argue with a straight face that my filth is better than
yours. A certain kind of daring is easier to muster these days.

At a two-day training session some months ago, I wrote
'shri' at the top of the first page of the writing pad given to us
and began taking notes. My hands shook as I wrote 'shri' with
two vertical lines on either side. A little later, I thought of the
superior types who lurk in disguise everywhere and scratched it
out while leaving the training venue.

Looking at these books makes me want to empty the
whole cabinet. As long as they are in front of me, they
will continue to remind me of my craving for some sort of

transformation. Even after all these years, I know that Viji sometimes discreetly asks questions to check if my thoughts are my own or something whispered in my ear by Tiwari. I don't let on that I know.

I finish my tea and open the cabinet. There is a mark near the edge of a shelf where one of us recently trailed a finger in the dust. A few assorted objects rest in the space in front of the books: a chipped mug stuffed with pens collected from meetings and conferences, old spectacles and their cases. On the second shelf are Rekha's tenth-standard textbooks for physics, chemistry and maths. Science books are harder to throw away. It feels as if their contents stay relevant forever. On the same shelf are books related to computer courses that Viji has done over the years. All the milestones we have passed as a family are in a way crammed into this showcase.

I bring a carton from the storage loft in the bathroom and begin filling it with books. This morning, when our whole building was crowded into our flat, I noticed second-floor Shivashankar engrossed in the contents of the cabinet. Maybe I can give them to him. But then, I don't know if he was looking at the books with genuine interest or if he was trying to judge me. Never mind. Easiest to keep the carton out of sight in the loft or give it to the scrap collector right away. I stuff dried-up pens and half-used notepads in the gaps between the books. The coins grow in a small heap on the floor. A bunch of bookmarks, held together by a sticky, melted rubber band, goes into the carton. That thick electrical engineering book must be somewhere in the house.

I don't touch Viji and Rekha's books. When I am done, the cabinet has only one of my books: *Living in Harmony.* Right next to Viji's copy of the book. This I cannot bring myself to get rid of.

I push the carton to one side of the room and wonder why I felt the need to do this just now. What am I trying to put off? *Why We Procrastinate* has just gone into the carton.

I walk about the house aimlessly. I am looking for some sign of disarray, some sort of stain. Something has happened here, but I don't know what. A sharp knife has been thrust in and removed so quickly that there is no trace of blood anywhere. I am waiting for the blood to spurt out and show me the wound.

I wander into Rekha's room. I had made up my mind to get her to talk about where she had gone, but the morning's commotion came in the way. She is writing a special report for that idiot Suresh's magazine it seems! Two losers feeding each other's delusions. What he writes goes viral on WhatApp it seems! I noticed that Rekha took her backpack with her to college. She explained away the uncles so easily – could it really be so straightforward? I am tired enough that I will accept any explanation that brings all of this to an end.

The door to her wardrobe is ajar. Nothing stands out in the room. I think of Ramana and how little he had. His entire world fit into a duffel bag and a cloth bag slung on one shoulder. He never left anything behind. And because there was nothing of his at home, he quickly faded from our memories. The only place he remained undiminished was in Amma's consciousness while she was alive. I don't recall Amma ever making buttermilk dosas after he was gone. I liked them too, but I never mustered the courage to ask for them. She wouldn't have made them in any case.

Tiredness catches up with me, and I go to the bedroom to lie down. I look at the almirah, the bunch of keys still dangling from it. I reach out to open it, check myself and again use a handkerchief to grasp the handle. I open both doors. The top half of the almirah is crowded with Viji's colourful saris on hangers. A single sleeve of my wedding suit peeps out from the rightmost corner. The bottom half has an entirely different design – three compartments on either side of a central partition. One is a locker, whose key is in the bunch. The thieves could easily have opened the locker. Maybe they did.

I try to size up the contents of the almirah through the eyes of the thieves. Our three passports are in a corner of the bottom-right compartment. We have never actually used them to travel abroad, but I get them renewed from time to time anyway. The same compartment has birth certificates, wedding papers, college marksheets and old bank passbooks. The family's entire financial history. Thankfully, they did not take any certificates. Otherwise, there would be endless running around to get duplicates. Where is the bundle with the flat's title deed? I keep it here somewhere. I peer into all the other compartments without finding it. So this is what they came for! I should call Viji and tell her. But wait, there in the bottom-right compartment at the back are all the house documents.

The saris are crammed together at the top of the almirah, and I move the hangers around a little to air them. A visiting card falls from the floor of this compartment to the ground. It's the carpenter's. I didn't think of looking for it here. How did it get here anyway?

The condoms are hidden behind the wall of saris. We knew, without having to discuss it, that we did not want another child. In the eyes of others, the first pregnancy appeared so carefully planned that Viji's mother's school closed for summer vacations the same week Rekha was born. From the outside such a coincidence is the same as foresight.

I am sure there's a certain charm to being overcome by desire and becoming pregnant by chance. But I have never had that kind of spontaneity. Ours has always been a polite, civilized intercourse, nothing too wild. Even in the heat of the moment, I unfailingly remembered to open the almirah and reach behind the saris. I have no doubt that Viji's 'It's okay, don't bother' was planned. And though we had not discussed it, I expected such a moment would come sooner or later and was prepared.

The intensity of a life can be measured in stupid decisions. I have always been envious of those who manage to be reckless. Maybe deep down I was envious of Ramana too.

It's impossible to rearrange the almirah without emptying it first. I clear the compartments one by one, placing their contents in heaps on the bed. In one of those heaps is an old drawing book that Rekha used as a child. Who knows how it got here. I flip through it and find two stick figures supposed to be me and Viji, with 'LOVE YOU' written below. I had felt a kind of happiness when Rekha had said 'I don't like her' about that CEO's daughter, what's her name, Sita. How good things are when our children depend on us for everything, how pleasant is their rebellion when it is within our control. But after a point, our own children end up becoming hot ghee in the mouth for us. After looking at a few mountains and trees, I place the book back on the bed. The locker. If we have anything valuable at home, this is where it will be. Right in front is a round steel tiffin box. Inside is Viji's mangalsutra. The mangalsutra's privilege from our honeymoon has not faded in my mind despite the intervening years. After we returned from Kodai, I never repeated the theatrical gesture of giving her my wallet. And I don't recall her ever hesitating before taking off her mangalsutra.

I look closely at the string of black beads in my hand – maybe it is cut, maybe the clasp is broken. A long time ago, when Viji was pregnant with Rekha, the beads of her mangalsutra were coming loose. She had taken it off without a fuss and handed it over to be repaired. She had bought a simple single-string replacement so her neck would not be bare. Maybe that is what she wears these days. I have not noticed her neck in a while. The mangalsutra must have slipped her mind when she said in the morning there was no gold in the house.

In the same box are the tiny silver bangles Rekha wore as a baby. This thing we call love, who knows how deep a disagreement it can withstand. Sometimes what feels like love is nothing more than duty. Maybe these feelings are best not examined too deeply. Do I really love anyone? Enough to give my life for them? But what does that mean anyway? What is left after life itself is given? There used to be a flower-seller named Bhavani in our village. When her little daughter slipped and fell into the tank, she jumped in after her despite not knowing how to swim. They both drowned.

Our possessions packed in the almirah's half-darkness appear more numerous when spread out on the bed, more ordinary when exposed to the light. It is as if the passage of time has drained away the feelings attached to these things. Now they are mere objects. We bought the almirah the year we got married. Its contents were acquired in the years that followed. The almirah holds only what we consider precious. But looking at these things now, the truth is that everything other than a few documents could have been taken away without making any real difference to our lives. If the intruders saw all this and did not touch anything, it clearly had no value in their eyes too.

I don't remember the context, but not so long ago, Rekha had said, 'Your lives are so ordinary.' I told her, 'Arre, most lives are ordinary.' Then, getting worked up a little, I said, 'You get everything you want. Life is comfortable. You went to one of the top schools of the city. There is nothing ordinary about any of that.' She taunted me with a superior little smile and said, 'I wasn't talking about money,' to let me know her definition of the ordinary was different.

I want to smash the likes of Suresh and Surendran to pieces. Feeding their self-importance by brainwashing young children. How else did these thoughts, these words, find their way into her mind? Suresh said her writing could be read on social media. I really should find her accounts and go through them carefully. I should make her understand that there is a difference between the Wadhwani girl and her. Perhaps she will call me a coward again as she did in the morning, this mad girl who wanted to change her name. It was from the plain-clothes policemen that we learnt that Ramana had gone by different names. Mohan. Sebastian. Rafique. Chandrahas. Ram Nair. The five names remain imprinted on my mind even though I only heard them that once. Was it easier for him to shoot someone as a Mohan or Sebastian? Did guilt not attach itself to actions committed under an assumed name? Maybe Rekha had a secret name as well. Asha or Natasha, Isabella or Jennifer.

A large pale-blue cover in the bottom-left compartment. It holds old office papers, pension documents, the appointment letter to my first job, a few increment letters. Self-appraisals going back twelve years, with the target in one column and what I achieved in the next. Looking at them now, both the targets and my results seem trivial. A single self-appraisal is enough to shatter a man's pride. They are designed to wear down a person's dignity by making him talk himself up. I once bought a book on how to write a powerful self-appraisal and read it secretly.

Amidst the office papers is a cream-coloured envelope. I have read the contents of the letter inside so often that I know them by heart. The letter is from Nila. Maybe she was Ramana's lover. Or wife. Or just comrade. From the letter it is clear she was convinced Ramana had told us about her. We had never heard her name before the letter arrived. Antanna bided his time on one of my visits to the village and handed the letter to me when there was no one else at home. All he said was, 'This came last week. It could be a police trick. Do as you see fit.' Nila wanted to visit the village and meet the family. The name on the envelope was Amma's. The address was minimal and precise, as if to certify that it had been given to her by Ramana himself. He had long been forgotten in our house when the letter arrived.

I brought the letter back with me from the village and went through it again and again when I was alone, trying to read between the lines. Unlike Ramana's handwriting, Nila's was neat. Her style was direct. She addressed Amma respectfully as Srimati Sundari and referred to her in the plural. Her tentativeness in addressing members of our family reflected the nature of her relationship with Ramana.

Nila said she wanted to visit our village to see Ramana's childhood home and his plantation. Did this imply he was alive somewhere? Or that he was not? How was it even possible to tell? People like this are capable of going underground for decades. She asked after everyone at home. She urged Amma to reply soon, but Amma and Appa had left us by then. The address she wrote from was on the Andhra border. What did she want from us?

I kept the letter in the almirah without telling anyone. No one would look through my office papers anyway. For some time after the letter arrived, I thought I must reach a decision about it. But to touch it was to hold a burning ember – such were the family politics, cruelty and perverse stubbornness tied up with it. It occurred to me that this Nila may have children by Ramana, that they may want a share of his property. Legally speaking, Ramana did not have an inch of land to his name. Appa made sure of that. What remained was a question of morals and sentiment. Nila had mentioned Ramana's plantation. Had Amma been alive she would have fought for Ramana's land to be handed over to her. But Amma was not alive. Was I to take up the responsibility of carrying out the instructions in his last letter? Who was Nila to me?

What Antanna said about the land after Ramana's last letter was deciphered still rings in my ears: 'We wouldn't have given it to him, as if we'll now give it to his whore. Ha.'

In the end I did nothing about the letter. Antanna never asked me about it again and I didn't mention it to Viji. Betrayal is easy when one cannot be found out.

I open the envelope and unfold the letter. The suspicion that someone else has read it flashes through my mind. Maybe it's just that I've been troubled since morning by the thought of strangers walking around the house. The two sheets of the letter had been folded lengthwise and across, and unless you folded it exactly along the already existing creases, it would sit uncomfortably in its envelope. As I hold it in my hand now, this letter that I have opened and read so many times feels strange to my eyes and fingers. I have already unfolded it, so there's no way to check how it was placed in the envelope. At the same time, I can't ignore the possibility that someone has read the letter. When I fold the letter as usual, it resists just a little, as if it has forgotten how.

The land by the tank has turned out to be an enormous python that has encircled us. With time its grip has only become tighter. We may have burnt Ramana's letter the very next day, but it never really went away. If she knew Ramana was dead, Amma would have managed to carry on somehow. But not knowing, and the thousand possibilities that then remained, snatched away her sleep.

* * *

After I finished my first semester exams and returned to the village, I was shocked to see how gaunt Amma had become. When I chided her for not eating properly, she said, 'It doesn't matter how much I eat. Nothing reaches the body when the mind is in pain. Everything goes there.'

Amma's day began with her entering the kitchen. After she had given us breakfast and finished her work there, she would tend to the plants in the backyard for an hour or two, bathe and then step into the puja room. It was only after completing her prayers that she served us lunch. A short while before she called us, we would hear the sounds of plates and lids from the kitchen. If something was being fried, its smell would begin to spread through the house. Two days after I returned for my holidays, I remember it was a Monday, Amma didn't call us for lunch though it was well past the usual time. I went and looked into the puja room. She was stretched out on the ground with her hands joined, as if she was prostrating herself in front of god, except her head was turned to one side and resting on the ground. I rushed to her. She was snoring softly. I didn't know if she was asleep or if she had fainted. 'Amma,' I said, touching her gently. She opened her eyes, took a moment to find her bearings and got up. She must have been embarrassed to have fallen asleep in the middle of the day. She tried to pretend as if nothing out of the ordinary had happened. I could only imagine how deprived of sleep she must have been to have fallen asleep on the ground like that.

Appa appeared as we both entered the kitchen. She said to him in an accusatory tone, 'He would have stayed at home if you had given him his land. Then he would not have fallen into bad company. We would still have him.'

Appa offered his old argument, his voice impatient: 'How many times did I say that I would make the land over to him the day he decided to stay here. Did he come?'

'Whatever he does, the right thing is to give him what is his.'

Appa raised his voice: 'We poured our blood into that plantation. He will ruin it in a day.'

Amma screamed: 'It is not yours. It is his. It is only his. It's a sin for us to keep it.'

I felt such words must have been spoken in the house before. Perhaps it was Amma's intention to say them in front of me.

'When he comes again, I will hand it over. Let him do whatever he wants and go to hell.'

'Did you hear him? Did you hear him?' Amma asked me. I did not say anything.

I don't know why she didn't realize that Antanna and Appa would never transfer the land to Ramana. That plantation was the most precious of our assets. Since it was close to the tank, the soil was exceptionally fertile. The plantation had two wells, from both of which water had gushed out when they dug down to barely twenty feet. Arecanut, pepper, cardamom – almost anything took when it was planted here. Had Antanna the slightest intention of returning the land, he would not have worked so hard on it.

Amma said, 'It should be according to his wishes. Either give it to the girl or distribute it among the workers. Whatever it is, we shouldn't keep it.'

'What if he shows up later and asks for the land? "Give it to the girl" it seems. We don't even know her name. And I'd go crazy before I would give it away to workers.'

I never expected Ramana to return. Though we received no such news, my impression was that the police had finished him

off. Appa and Antanna though insisted to Amma that he was
sure to come home one day. All kinds of stories about Ramana
floated around the village. It was impossible to take his name
outside the walls of our house. Visits from Amma's side of the
family stopped entirely. Some people must have heard what he
intended for his land when his last letter was read in public.
It was why Antanna had leapt up to snatch the letter from
Gurudasa's hands.

Though Amma never mentioned Ramana's land to Viji,
she made sure that the thorn of that particular obligation
pricked us from within. After she was gone, no one spoke of
it again.

* * *

Nila's letter in my hand is an invitation to disaster. Best to erase
this history completely. I tear the letter into small pieces and
stuff them back in the envelope. I will throw it in the office
dustbin tomorrow. I tuck the envelope into the bag I carry to
work. But what if whoever read the letter also photographed it?
I push the thought away even as I begin to feel uneasy.

I move on to the lower compartments of the almirah.
A small carved sandalwood box that came to us as a wedding
gift. We kept it in the almirah thinking it would impart its
fragrance to everything inside, but when its smell faded with
time, we realized it was an ordinary wooden box smeared with
a little sandalwood oil. But it stayed in its place. The box holds
three voter ID cards and a bank locker key. The scenes we
witnessed at home during the election two months ago! It was
the first time Rekha voted.

With around fifteen days to go for the election, one of the candidates from our constituency, Shankar Rao, made some controversial comments about how girls should dress. This became linked to matters of Indian culture and so on, and became a subject of heated discussion on the evening news shows. The three of us were watching the shouting matches as we ate dinner, with Rekha becoming increasingly agitated. Rao's features and his protruding teeth did not make him the most pleasant-looking politician. Rekha couldn't control her rage after watching endlessly looping clips of Rao's words. She burst out, through clenched teeth: 'What is wrong with this creepy uncle? Just look at his ugly face.'

It astonishes me now to think how the exchanges between the three of us escalated from there.

Viji was initially silent, but later came down on Rekha's side. There was nothing new to any of this. I ignored them and silently watched the TV. At some point, Rekha said, 'Appa, why aren't you saying anything?'

'What is there to say? I'm just watching quietly.'

'I know why you're quiet.'

'Why?'

'You support that buck-toothed baboon, that's why.'

'Think about it a little,' I said. 'He has already won twice. People say he does at least some good work. We should look at the context in which he said those things. What we should not do is make fun of someone for their appearance. I don't like it.'

'So you agree with what he said?'

'These things are not black and white. If I agreed with him, would I last another minute in this house?'

She pounced upon this last comment. 'So we are the only reason you don't support him. What would you do left to yourself?'

'Don't take his statements so seriously. These things are routine during elections.'

'It is because we remain quiet that such people get elected.'

'Tell me how we should oppose it. By sitting here at the dining table and arguing?'

For a moment Rekha was at a loss. But she did not give up. 'We could talk about it with people we know. We could go to every house in our building and make them aware of the issue.'

'Aiyo, Putti. Political change doesn't happen because people hold a certain opinion. You all won't understand this now. Pay attention to your studies and finish college. You can think about politics later.' I knew she did not like to be called Putti, especially during a serious discussion.

Rekha was fuming. 'What do you mean I don't understand? Of course I understand.'

Viji joined in. 'How about telling us just who is included in your "you all"?'

It took some effort on my part to convey that I had not meant it as a slight to all women.

I guessed that Rekha's political opinions had come from her hero, Surendran, and this presented itself as a good opportunity to dig into him. I had cast a couple of stones this way, and while I was at it, I might as well toss one that way too. But I managed to exercise restraint and that was where it ended – for that day.

At office the next day, a colleague named Gunashekhar launched into a passionate speech at the lunch table, justifying why he was going to vote for Shankar Rao's party. His view sounded reasonable to me. He said, 'I have two daughters. You should see the clothes they wear. I am terrified something will happen to them when they go out. I have no peace of mind until they return. But what can I say to them? My wife takes their side, and if I bring it up, they all pounce on me together. Now that a political party is saying openly what I cannot say at home, my vote is definitely for them.'

Another colleague, Vinod, heard this and spoke up, bursting Gunashekhar's balloon: 'Guna-bhai, this was on one of my WhatsApp groups. The message asked people with daughters to share it with others, making it out to be their own experience. How convincing you were! You deserve an award for both your acting and for being a true believer.'

Gunashekhar tried to justify himself. 'How does the source matter? Isn't what I am saying true?'

Vinod went on: 'It gives off a rotten smell when personal matters like the clothes people wear become politicized. However tightly anyone closes their doors and windows, it enters everyone's house.'

'Maybe it won't be noticed because of the fragrance the other parties have been spreading,' Gunashekhar said.

Everyone laughed. Vinod kept quiet after that.

I had no intention of bringing up this discussion at home. But that very day a rowdy harassed a young woman on the street, was caught and beaten up by the public. When questioned, he said he had been provoked by her clothes. The TV channels, finding no greater issue of national importance, chose this incident to dissect endlessly in their studios. It reminded me of the conversation at lunch, and I recounted a carefully worded version of it.

Even as I spoke, I realized that the embers from the previous evening not only remained alive but were actually being fanned by what I was saying. Gunashekhar was not a stranger to us. He had visited us with his wife and daughters. But now Rekha and Viji roasted him on the flame of their words, dabbing a little masala about the self-importance of men, the mentality that allowed them to trample all over women and so on.

Viji brought up her cousin Anagha's story. 'Anagha's husband's business is thriving apparently. Now that he has a little money, he creates a scene daily, asking her to leave her teaching job. He says he will pay her what she is earning. She is not supposed to wear anything other than saris. He says such ugly things when he talks about politics that she says she feels like vomiting. One day, when she tried to argue with him, he forwarded her some crazy WhatsApp message, then snatched her phone and forwarded it to all her contacts to embarrass her. She's disgusted she has to sleep with the man and feels like throwing up every time he touches her. She cried a lot the other day, saying why did my life turn out like this.'

'Her husband is Anand, no? Who used to come to our house on a red bike? Amma, how did he become like this?'

'He didn't become anything. Such people have always been like this. She should have seen the signs before getting married.'

'What are the signs?'

'So much patriotism that they have to flare out their chest and thump it.'

'They are always looking for new enemies.'

'They love to puff up their cheeks and blow a conch.'

'If there's still any doubt, you should pay attention to the things they say.'

Mother and daughter began to list these things.

'If my parents agree I have no objection.'

'You should be proper first. Complain about men later.'

'Know your place.'

Rekha turned serious and said to her mother, 'Anagha should leave him, Amma.'

'They have kids.'

'So what?'

'Children are a noose around a woman's neck. It tightens when she leaves her husband.'

Their talk stopped here. Heat from the volcano inside had begun to radiate. I had given up and resolved to keep my mouth shut no matter what the provocation. There was an undercurrent in their words that suggested I was in agreement with such villains. I kept my eyes fixed on the TV screen, flipping through channels with the remote in my hand. One of the news channels had a mighty commotion in progress under the pretext of discussing women's clothes, Indian culture, safety and incidents of harassment. This was a channel none of us could stand. Even when it came on by mistake, we changed it as quickly as possible. As usual, it had spokespersons from several political parties and organizations all simultaneously shouting whatever came into their heads. People with opposing viewpoints seemed to be invited just so they could pour ghee into the flames. This time I stayed on the channel.

The TV's clamour filled our hall. Words that had never been heard in our house now ran through it in a torrent. Mother and daughter were both appalled. Maybe they thought I was letting these television warriors loose on them to watch the fun. I pretended to be absorbed in what was happening on the TV. This must have annoyed them further.

'Why are you listening to these thugs?'

'We should know both sides of the argument.'

'Isn't it enough to hear it once? They're vomiting the same thing again and again in different ways.'

'It's not good to be so intolerant. What is wrong in hearing them out?'

'And today of all days! Listen to them all night if you want. I can't take it for one more second.' Viji stormed off to the bedroom. Rekha followed her.

I heard Tiwari say: You are your own best friend. Love yourself first, then share what is left. I stayed firm. I watched until the discussion was over and went in to sleep. The light in our room was off and Viji was lying down facing away from me. She said, 'You know everything that comes out of their mouths is shit. Did you want to see how much there is?'

'See how the two of you have turned a small matter into something big.'

'A small matter!'

I was elated by the disgust in her tone. This was the perverse pleasure of having gained the upper hand. I had been adamant about watching that channel, and it felt like the victory of someone who may be caught for corruption but manages to hang on to the ill-gotten gains anyway. What fault could they possibly find in wanting to hear out the other side? I had beaten them with their own stick. At one point that evening, when their words were flying around like bullets, she had turned to me and said, 'Why are you smiling?'

A smile must have inadvertently formed on my lips as I had thought to myself: 'All they can do is sit here and talk. The reality outside is very different.' Just the other day, after the uncles had left, Viji had said there was another man inside me. It must have been he who supplied the cruelty required for such a smile. And it must have been he who made me bring up in this context the matter of Susan, my classmate from junior college. She was from Goa and the only girl who came to college wearing a skirt. The boys in my class, who didn't have the courage to so much as look at any other girl, never shied away from talking to her. Viji and Rekha were revolted. It is possible I had a smile on my face when they fell upon me saying, 'So if she wears a skirt, she becomes easy? Chee!' The picture that came to my mind was that of a ringmaster who ignores the roars of a lion and continues to prod it with his stick to show off his dominance.

The next few days went by with a strange tension in the air. The skirmishes at home continued – through implied barbs, words muttered to oneself and things said under the veil of the right to express a different opinion. One evening, Rekha gave me an order: 'Appa, whatever you do, don't vote for that baboon.'

I said, 'All right, Putti. As you say.'

My submission to her was like the weakness one feigns while wrestling with a child. She scowled. When I prodded a bit, it turned out there was a rumour going around college about a dress code to be imposed from the next month, and the girls were upset about it. She said, 'Some of the college administrative council members are supporters of that fellow. We know whom they are targeting. None of us will stay quiet if they try to do something. The best time for such ideas to be nipped in the bud is during an election.'

I suspected it was Surendran who had made the connection between the dress code and the upcoming elections. It was not possible for Rekha to know how the invisible tentacles of the system were spread, and which spark could burn down what. It must be his work. Rekha naively believed that her vote could change everything. If I tried to educate her about how the world worked, she would perceive it as cynicism. I did not try.

We set out together on the day of the election. Our voting booth was at a school about ten minutes' walk away. As soon as we left Rekha cautioned me: 'Appa, you know what to do.'

I laughed and asked, 'Who are you voting for?'

'It's confidential. But you know who I am not voting for.'

'If he votes for that Rao, I will leave him. What do you say?' Viji said, looking to her daughter as if for support.

'I'll join you. Can't live in the same house with traitors. When the knot is cut, the noose cannot tighten.'

'Poor Anagha. Such a sad story.'

'Votes are kept secret so that families stay together,' I said. They both laughed. Though I'd meant it as a joke, I couldn't help thinking just how much can be bound up in a vote. If everything that went into a vote was teased apart, what stories could emerge from each one! A vote might contain the glow of virtue needed to sleep with one's wife or the torment of a woman compelled to give her body to a husband she loathed. Who knew what unsaid things deep inside found expression in a vote? The only thing we can be sure of is that a vote is not as straightforward as it seems.

We reached the school that had our voting booth and stood in line inside the compound. A large poster showed the names of candidates and their symbols. The second name was Shankar Rao.

Rekha went in first. Then Viji. When I entered, all three of us were in different stages of casting our vote in a single large room. The electronic ballot box was hidden from view by a makeshift cardboard partition. I watched Rekha walk up to it. I could only see the top of her head over the partition. Then Viji. After they both went out, it was my turn.

I got my finger inked, entered the cardboard enclosure and stood there alone. For a moment I was flustered. It scared me to think that no one other than me would know what I did here. My hand faltered under the weight of this freedom. My heart pounded. I looked at the names and symbols next to the buttons on the machine's panel.

One of the voting booth officials called out: 'Sir, any problem?'

I shook my head to say no and plunged my finger into the button. I left without giving it any more thought. My face was covered in sweat. I took a moment to recover so that Viji and Rekha wouldn't notice my state. I found them waiting for me by the school's gate.

The results came after a week. Rao had won. Sitting in front of the TV, Rekha raged: 'That fool! And those who voted for him are worse.' Viji was on her side. I looked at Rekha's downcast face and felt sorry for her.

'Amma, thousands of people have voted for him. Maybe half are men. And let's say half of these men are married. What must be the plight of their wives?'

Viji said, 'Some like Anagha's husband don't hide who they are. In those cases we know what we are dealing with. Worse are those who eat cow dung on the sly and say they didn't while their mouth stinks.'

I put the voter ID cards back in the sandalwood box and place the box on the bed. Didn't a minister say some nonsense recently about cow dung being an antiseptic? I hold back a laugh. For some reason, Viji's recent behaviour towards me flashes in front my eyes. Among everything else, the way she pulled her hand away from mine in the bus. What if I had grabbed it by force? I should have. A woman can make a scene if a stranger touches her in a bus. But what can she do when it's her husband?

It's too much, all these memories leaping up at me. I make some room on the bed and lie down. My back sinks into the mattress and my muscles relax. I realize just how exhausted I am. I ignore the contents of the almirah pressing against my sides and thighs and stretch out my legs. I look at the ceiling and think of how films portray a person's entire existence in two hours. Maybe my life story can be told through the act of tidying up this almirah. Everything needed for transitions and flashback scenes is right here. Degree certificates, a mangalsutra, a photo of my parents, Nila's letter, the voter ID cards. Among scenes with strong narrative potential, one is definitely the mangalsutra's privilege. Then, the hunt for Rekha and the election in which she cast her first vote. Is there anything that makes for a good cliffhanger at the interval? Where does Ramana fit in? The film should capture the ominous signs quietly present around routine, everyday activities. As well as the helplessness born of being unable to comprehend them. The cruelty of the uncles must find a place. Is it necessary to throw in the stupid lovesick boy? How can the kind of politics that sows imaginary fears and sets people at each other's throats be shown? For those who think everything can be understood, there should be a clear resolution to Rekha's disappearance. There are any number of possibilities for an exciting twist. Maybe Rekha reads Nila's letter and sets out to find her? Is that far-fetched? As I imagine the scenes unfold it seems quite plausible. What if Rekha had set out to make her life extraordinary? After all, Suresh was there to instigate her. Something like this would be a big deal for his little rag. What were mother and daughter whispering about in the afternoon yesterday? Just how much did Viji know? What if Rekha had gone in search of Ramana himself?

Or, or . . . What if Rekha told Suresh about Nila's letter? That rogue is capable of getting someone to impersonate her. He knows there is no way to verify her identity. No one has seen her even. Anyone and anything can be made true with the might of the media. And what if this foolish girl, with all her craving for revolution and justice, simply hands over the plantation to a fake Nila? Suresh knows very well the worth of four acres of fertile land. As well as the ins and outs of dealing with inherited property. Even as my imagination wanders, my eyes begin to pull themselves shut.

When I wake up, I cannot tell for how long I have slept. I didn't get much sleep the last two nights. I have not had lunch, but sleep won over hunger. From the silence in the house I can tell that Viji and Rekha have not yet returned. It is almost dark. I was thinking of cinema scenes before I drifted off. My sleeping amidst these objects will make for a good overhead shot. Seen suddenly from above, the scene might appear like one of Ramana's letters. A rectangular bed, just like a page, and on it, like Ramana's crows-feet-sparrows-feet writing, a jumble of things, including me waiting to be assigned meaning.

A knock at the door. I am dimly aware there has already been such a knock. It is what woke me up. If it is the police, they will want a list of missing items. None of the responses I can think of feels right.

Nothing is missing.

We don't know what is missing.

We are still looking. If we find out what we're missing, I will come to the police station myself.

I imagine the disbelief on their faces after hearing my statement and wonder what consequences it can bring.

What if it is not the police but those uncles from the other day? Or, what if it is the police, but here for something else? Or is it someone else entirely?

I get up and turn on the light.

More knocking. I curse their impatience and go to the door.

* * *

Acknowledgements

The author thanks Gayatri Prabhu, Nikhil Govind and the Manipal Centre for Humanities, where he worked on parts of this book as writer-in-residence.

The author and translator thank their agents, Shruti Debi and Anna Stein; Elizabeth Kuruvilla and Saloni Mital at Penguin Random House India; and Aisling Brennan and Libby Marshall at Faber.